GUNS · GRIT · N · WOMEN

A Collection of Short Western Stories

R. Orin Vaughn

LIVIN' THE WILD WEST
CODY, WY 2018
Orin Vaughn

ISBN-13: **978-1495970481**

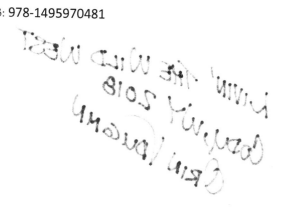

DEDICATION

I have published this book of Western Short Stories myself in the belief that there are still those out there who appreciate a Western written in the Classic, Traditional Style. No, I do not claim to be the quality of writer as those before me, who you and I admire. However, neither do I want their style and tradition to be forgotten or lost.

Volumes and volumes of Western Stories have been written and read, some GREAT, others not so great. Western books have been given as gifts, passed around, traded, and sold at yard sales and to used bookstores. Still, they are picked up by a *select few* and read and reread and passed around again.

So, hopefully here are some New Stories for you, with the same flavor that some of us still appreciate.

Yours truly,
R. ORIN VAUGH

CONTENTS

ACKNOWLEDGMENTS

My sincere thanks and appreciation goes first to my good friend Michael Brose, then to my mother-in-law Carol, my son Lucas and last but certainly not least to my dear wife Julie. Without their support and encouragement this book may never have been published.

I also want to express my appreciation to those whose personalities and experiences contributed to some of the unique characters and story lines in this collection.

.

THE DEATH OF AUGUST PITT

Ever since Julie could remember, Grandpa Bud and Mom Lois made a yearly trip up to the mountains to visit the old ghost town of Chase, and every year she had begged to go along, but never once had he given in and let her go, or anyone else for that matter. It was only Grandpa Bud and Mom Lois that would make the trip.

Bud Paxton had been the town marshal up there a long time ago before buying the ranch. No one knew for sure why he and his wife would go up that hard, unforgiving, mountain road to that old ghost town. He didn't talk much about his days there, but he would never miss the trip for any reason.

It was July 10, 1920 and Bud was packing for the annual trip. Grandpa Bud was what all the children at the ranch affectionately called this gruff, yet gentle man named, Bud Paxton. Grandpa Bud and his wife, Mom Lois, as she was known to the children, owned a fifty-five acre ranch about twenty-five miles northwest of Phoenix, Arizona. The ranch was named "The Molly Rhodes Ranch Home for Children", it was named after the woman that ran the orphanage where Bud had grown up. The ranch itself was sort of an orphanage and school for abandoned and unwanted children. Unlike other places of its kind in these days, the people who ran it, Bud Paxton and wife Lois, were the sweetest and nicest people that you would ever want to know. Sure, the children had their chores, and they worked hard, but they were dearly loved and cared for, each and every one.

Julie, a baby girl rescued by her father from a hotel fire in San Francisco, was put in the arms of a maid. Then the father rushed back in to save his wife. However, he didn't make it back and perished in the fire. All the hotel records had been destroyed and no one knew Julie's identity. The baby was estimated to be around three months old at the time of the fire. After an advertising campaign in the newspapers failed to identify any relatives, a woman who knew of the ranch brought the baby out to the ranch, and the Paxton's took her in without hesitation.

After about a year Bud and Lois Paxton adopted the baby girl. They named her Julie, after the baby girl they had lost at birth years before. Bud Paxton never felt it was right to keep the truth from Julie about her adoption. He wanted her to know the truth about herself and felt it was the same as lying not to tell her. So Julie knew how she came to be with the Paxton's and she never questioned the situation and she always considered Grandpa Bud and Mom Lois to be her mother and father. Like everyone else, Julie called them Mom Lois and Grandpa Bud.

Usually a neighbor or friend would come out to the ranch and help watch over the children, who generally numbered fourteen or fifteen. Grandpa Bud and Mom Lois would be gone three or four days, staying at the hotel in the relocated town of Chase, about ten miles down the mountain from its original location. This year, Mom Lois would not be able to make the trip with Grandpa Bud to the mountains. Prominent businessmen from Phoenix had made a commitment to supply funding for the ranch and they were sending two representatives the next day to look things over. Someone had to be there and Grandpa Bud had made it clear it certainly wasn't going to be him.

This was going to be Julie's last summer at the ranch since she had turned eighteen and would be going off to college in the fall. She wanted to be a teacher, but beyond college she wasn't sure where she would go. Julie was a bright girl and had been granted a full scholarship at a small college in southern Illinois.

Mom Lois and Grandpa Bud were in the kitchen discussing his trip when Julie walked in and interrupted their conversation.

"Oh, Grandpa Bud," Julie pleaded, batting her long lashes over her sparkling light blue persuasive eyes. "Pl-ease let me go with you this time since Mom Lois can't go?"

"I am sorry Julie. It's simply out of the question," he said.

"And, tell me why not, Bud Paxton?" said Lois.

"You know I don't take anybody up there with me, except you," he replied, "and that's because you're...you're my wife."

"Well, Julie's your daughter," Lois said. "She has a right to know what you're all about."

"Yeah. Maybe," said Bud.

Grandpa Bud turned his attention to Julie. "You know I love you dearly. I just don't want to take anyone other than Mom up there."

"Oh, come on," Julie hugged his arm. "I won't be any trouble, I promise. Besides, what's up there that I can't know about?" Julie looked at him with trusting eyes. "I love you no matter what," she assured him.

"See what you've done Mom," said Bud. His resolve softened as he ran his fingers through Julie's golden hair. "Now, how am I going to get this girl off my arm?"

Julie laid her face on his arm and tightened her grip. "And...She can't stay in the same hotel room with me. People will talk. What about that?"

"Oh now come on. She's your daughter for Pete sake Bud," said Lois. "Besides, if you're worried about that you can stay up at the lodge on the lake. Those cabins have three bedrooms. Your old buddy, Mack Henry, will give you a good rate and you know it."

Bud frowned, "Mack talks too much," he said. "You got all the answers, don't you?"

"Yes," she said, "Yes I do as a matter of fact. As long as you got questions, I got answers."

After some thought and a long look at Lois, who was standing with her hand on her hip, he said, "We-l-l what are you waiting for gal? Go get your bag packed."

"You mean...you mean I can go?"

"Only if you're ready when I am," he said. Julie rushed out of the kitchen eager to get ready. She could hardly believe she was really going. Bud turned back to his wife and said, "I hope this isn't a big mistake."

"You worry too much Bud Paxton," Lois said. "That girl loves you and always will. I understand why you have a need to go up there at this time, and if it comes out, Julie will understand too."

The next morning after loading the 1915 model "center door" Cadillac (It had been donated to the ranch by a rich uncle of Lois', who was a movie producer.) Bud and Julie headed out on the road north to the small mountain town of Chase. It was a six-hour drive from the ranch up some rough mountain roads.

Julie was so excited that her nerves came out of her mouth and she just jabbered on. She realized after a while that Grandpa Bud was in a solemn mood, for he was exceptionally quiet as he drove. Though she didn't understand it, she figured it would be a good idea to go along with his mood. Julie settled back and watched the scenery go by, napping off and on until they got there.

It had been a long tiring drive when they finally pulled in at the lodge on the lake. Mack Henry came out of the office and greeted Bud with an overly hardy handshake. Then, they had some small talk about the good old days when he had been marshal. Julie had been left in the car and Grandpa Bud didn't bother to introduce her as she expected he would. That wasn't like him and she wondered why he hadn't.

Mack Henry was a short older fellow that seemed to laugh a lot when there wasn't really anything to laugh about. At one point in his conversation with Grandpa Bud he pointed over at Julie sitting in the car. After Grandpa Bud said something, Mack looked over and laughed. With a prune-faced-grin, showing he didn't have a tooth in his head, he said, "Howdy Julie. Pleased ta meet ya."

Julie smiled and said, "Hello." Not long after that Grandpa Bud got back in the car with Julie and drove to a roomy log cabin up on a peaceful hillside covered with tall pines.

They unpacked and fixed some supper from the things they had brought along. Bud, maintained his quite spirit through the meal. It just wasn't like him. Then after supper he said, "Well we'd better hit the sack early tonight. It's gonna be a long day tomorrow and I want to get an early start." When the supper dishes were washed and put away, Bud read a couple of chapters out of the Bible as he usually did before bed.

In the morning before Julie woke up, Bud had two rented horses and gear ready for the ride up to the ghost town. The old mountain road was rocky and deeply cut by former years of wagon traffic. Riding leisurely, they traveled past majestic balancing rock formations to the site of the original town of Chase. Julie found it hard to believe that anyone would really build a town in such a rugged place in the mountains. They had though, because of the rich deposit of silver found there by Philip Gordon Chase.

When the ground leveled out they rode slowly down what used to be the main street of town. Now, it was grown over in high grass and less than a dozen buildings still lined the street. Those that stood were not much more than dried out shells of what they once were.

Her thoughts wandering, Julie visualized people on the street going about their daily business. She imagined a storekeeper sweeping the boardwalk, looking up and smiling as they passed. They passed by a row of gutted buildings with faded lettering identifying three of them as saloons. She heard ghostlike sounds of laughter, piano music and men joking with dance hall girls at the gambling tables coming from inside.

Julie looked over to ask a question of Grandpa Bud, his solemn look was even more noteworthy than it had been in the car the night before. The thought of her question slipped away as she noticed his arduous scowl.

When they reached the far edge of town, Julie realized where his attention had been fixed. A crumbling stone and wrought iron fence surrounded the town's cemetery. Bud reined his horse over to a patch of yellow and purple wild flowers growing abundantly just outside the cemetery entrance. He dismounted and picked a large handful and arranged them in somewhat of a bouquet.

"Come on Julie," he said, "Follow me. I'll show you why I come up here every year."

Julie stepped down off her mount and after they tied off the horses, Bud led Julie into the cemetery to a double gravesite. One of the grave markers was as worn and run down as the rest in the cemetery, but the other was fairly well kept in comparison. Julie looked at the engraving on the marker. It read:

IN LOVING MEMORY
OF
MOLLY L. RHODES – PITT
A WOMAN LOVED DEARLY BY
EVERYONE WHO KNEW HER
BORN NOV 1836 – DIED OF THE FEVER
JULY 11TH 1875

Julie realized July eleventh was the date today. "Molly Rhodes?" questioned Julie thoughtfully.

"This is the lady that the ranch is named after, isn't it? You thought a lot of her didn't you Grandpa Bud?"

"Yes I did," he answered. "Outside of Mom Lois she was the nicest, kindest woman I ever knew."

Julie looked at the eroded engraving on the grave marker next to Molly's. It read:

MARSHAL AUGUST J. PITT
BORN – – – – DIED JULY 14TH 1875
KILLED BY A STRANGER OVER A
THREE LEGGED DOG

Julie raised an inquisitive eyebrow and said, "Molly had a husband who was the Marshal?"

"Yes she did, and he was a no good, low down...We-l-l, let's just say he wasn't a nice fellow, that's all."

"Killed over a dog three days after Molly died? Why? Who did it?" asked Julie.

"Well, that's a long story and I'm not sure you need to hear of it anyway," said Grandpa Bud.

"I do. Come on Grandpa Bud, I want to know what happened. Come on now, you can't bring me all the way up here and show me Molly's grave and not tell me the story behind these head stones. What happened to Molly's husband?

"You had something to do with it, didn't you? That's why you didn't want me to come up here," said Julie.

"It was a stranger," said Bud. "Probably Billy Mason." Bud shook his head as he mumbled, "That dog-gone stonecutter Foley. He thought he had to chisel a story book on every gravestone he made."

"Who is Billy Mason? What's he got to do with this? You just have to tell me the story now," Julie insisted.

The excitement in Julie's eyes told him that she wasn't going to let it rest, and saying no to Julie wasn't something Bud Paxton found easy to do.

So reluctantly he motioned with his hand and said, "Come with me". He led Julie over to another gravesite. "He swallowed hard as he looked down on the marker. He just couldn't keep himself out of trouble."

This marker read:

BILLY MASON
BORN MAY 17TH 1854 – DIED JULY
23RD 1875
KILLED IN AN ATTEMPTED STAGE
HOLD UP
BELIEVED TO HAVE SHOT MARSHAL
AUGUST PITT

"Now," said Bud, "let's get the sandwiches we brought and sit in the shade of that tree yonder by the gate. Then, I'll tell you a little about old Chase back in the days when I was a youngster."

The horses were grazing contentedly and Bud loosened the saddles while Julie spread a blanket and set out the picnic lunch for them.

As they ate and enjoyed the peacefulness of the mountain quiet Bud began the story about his childhood in Chase.

He started, "Miss Molly." he paused, his lip tightened, and his brow wrinkled as his strong weathered face held back the flood of emotion spilling out from his eyes.

He made a fist and forced himself to relax a bit, then started again. "Yes, Miss Molly. Everyone called her that, even after she was married. She answered an ad in a newspaper and came all the way from Texas to become Chase's first schoolteacher. After settling in at her new job and getting accustomed to the town, she became aware of a number of children with no parents or anyone to really care for them. Molly, being the kind hearted soul she was and having a great love of children, started taking them in and feeding them. Some local people donated bedding and clothing and it wasn't long before she was running a sort of orphanage.

"You see, my situation was somewhat like yours, Julie," he explained. "My parents had been killed in an Indian raid up around Sand Creek. My mother had hidden me in the smokehouse and a passing trapper heard me crying. I wasn't quite two years old then. The trapper brought me to Molly's orphanage and that is where I stayed until I was fourteen. About that same time a young lad had been abandoned by a saloon girl when she ran off with some gambler. He was around the same age as I was. His name was Billy Mason. He and I grew up together and we were like brothers, we even looked a somewhat alike." Bud sighed, "Billy and I both loved animals and gladly took care of the few we had there at Molly's place.

"Molly was kind and loving and the townsfolk were generous. We even did pretty well during the Civil War years. It was a good life at the orphanage, that is, until August Pitt blew into town one afternoon."

Bud shifted slightly on the blanket. Julie looked up at him and her heart froze. Grandpa Bud had clenched his jaws so tight, she could see the muscles bulging. His eyes were burning red with hatred at just the mention of, August Pitt. Julie had never seen him this way before. All the loving warmth of Grandpa Bud was gone and a stranger now sat across from her. A feeling of fear came over Julie and she could only watch and wait for the whole story.

Drawing in a ragged breath and scowling, he continued. "Pitt had been wounded in some famous battle and convinced people that he was somewhat of a war hero. He loved limping around town telling his story over and over to all that would listen. A lot of people in the town admired him, but a few saw him as he really was a drunken braggart and a just plain mean man.

"Pitt became totally infatuated with Miss Molly the first time he laid eyes on her. He would go out of his way to meet up with her on the street and then put on his best manners and charm whenever he talked with her. Being young and naive Molly didn't see through his facade, though most of us kids did. He started coming round regular at the orphanage. Molly would invite him for supper, and it did seem like he was a decent sort when he was around her.

"Molly was impressed by his charm, but she hadn't seen him in the saloons with his friends, drinking and bragging. Pitt never came to the orphanage with alcohol on his breath, that is, before he convinced Molly to marry him. It wasn't long after they were married though, that he began to show his true nature.

"He would come home drunk and cuss at the children for being in his way. At first, when Molly would speak up, he would just curse under his breath and go to bed where he would pass out and sleep it off. The next day, Pitt would be nothing but apologies, and Molly would forgive him. That's just the way she was. It wouldn't be two days before it would all happen again though.

"Pitt began to hire out the children to do chores for the townsfolk. He explained that it was to raise money for the orphanage. Of course, the orphanage would never see a penny of that money and neither would Molly or any of the kids, Pitt would drink it up. Things were bearable, that is until one afternoon in midsummer." Pausing, Bud opened a canteen of water, took a sip and spat it on the ground. He gazed out at the ruins of the town remembering what it once was and the events that took place there.

The horses were grazing contentedly and she wanted him to continue, but dared not say a word. As he tightened the cap on the canteen he began again. "Two rowdy drifters came into town and refused to abide by the new town ordinance to check their guns at the Marshal's Office. Someone informed the Marshal, but only after the drifters had enough time to get pretty well liquored up.

When the Marshal came in and confronted the two, they refused to hand over their pistols. Instead they drew down and shot him. Pitt was in the saloon when the Marshal was shot. As the marshal hit the floor, Pitt slipped his boot knife out and planted it in the back of one of the drifters. Using the injured man as cover, Pitt grabbed his pistol and shot the other man dead. Pitt then finished off the man he had stabbed with the man's own pistol. In some people's eyes this qualified Pitt as a genuine town hero.

"The marshal died three days later of his wounds. Pitt being the town hero and with a little encouragement from some of his drinking buddies, who were influential men in town, the Town Council appointed Pitt as the new marshal.

"That only made things worse at the orphanage because, now that he had a standing in the town it went straight to his head. It wasn't long before he was bullying people and extorting protection money from them. Pitt kept law and order in Chase all right, and he was quick to remind the townspeople of that anytime they question him.

"His drunken homecomings were more often now and he began to slap Molly around. He would complain about what a rotten wife she was because she wouldn't have his supper ready, or he didn't like the way it was fixed. He didn't mind kicking a kid out of his way anytime he could either.

"Then came that night in the fall of sixty-eight, I remember it well. A local shopkeeper had given Billy and me this red pup. We took it home and begged Molly to let us keep it. She finally said yes, but only if we agreed to keep it out in the wood shed until she could clear it with August. He didn't like animals, not even horses.

"A storm was brewing that night and the thunder and lightning coming in was fierce. Billy and I heard the pup whimpering out in the woodshed. When we couldn't stand it any longer we got out of bed, dressed and slipped out to the shed. The plan was to sneak the pup into our bed and keep him quiet until the next morning, and then we would put him back outside when the storm was over. Trouble was Pitt caught us going into the house as he came home."

"What the hell is this?" said Pitt.

"Billy explained, 'It's our dog. Mr. McFarland gave him to Bud and me. We're gonna keep him.'"

"'Ya ain't keepin' no mangy mutt around here,' said Pitt as he snatched the pup out of Billy's arms and shoved him down. I made a grab for the pup, but Pitt saw me coming and met me with a backhand that sent me sprawling.

"Pitt held the pup up in the air by the scruff of its neck, looked at it disgustedly and said, 'Here… Ya want this sick lookin' piece of coyote bate. Then go get 'em.' With that he threw the pup across the lot and pulled his pistol.

"I jumped up and ran to stop him as he took aim. I was too late Pitt fired. Billy however had chucked a large rock at Pitt and it hit him in the head just as he fired the pistol.

"The .44 spoke loudly, nearly deafening me. The pup yelped in terrible agony. Pitt had shot one of the pup's front paws clean off.

"The impact of the rock sent Pitt stumbling back and he fell hard on his butt. Billy ran to the pup that was spinning in the dust violently, blood everywhere. It started to rain as thunder crashed and lightning lit up the night. Pitt's .44 was lying on the ground about three feet away from him. Billy and I both had the same thought as we looked at each other. Pitt was on his knees struggling to regain his senses.

"Billy shouted, 'Get the gun and shoot that drunken bum.'

"It was pouring rain and lighting was flashing all around. My ears were still ringing from the gun shot blast and the loud claps of thunder. It was difficult to focus as I walked over and picked up the pistol. I remember the gun being surprisingly heavy. I had seen people shoot pistols before and realized I had to cock the hammer back, so I did. Pitt looked up at me as I raised the pistol with both hands and pointed it at his head. Blood and rain ran down his forehead into his eyes. He glared at me with an evil grin that pierced my very soul and dared, 'Go ahead ya little runt, pull that trigger... Ya ain't got the guts, do ya? Yer a little yellow runt, just like that pup.'

"'Go ahead,' Billy yelled with hateful tears in his eyes. 'Go on, kill him.'

"I was confused by the ringing in my ears and my emotions were running wild as tears began to fill my eyes." Grandpa Bud's cold expression said he was reliving the experience. He stared off into the distance as he paused before continuing. "Pitt was right I didn't have the guts to shoot. I stuck the pistol in my belt and turned and ran. Billy, with the pup wrapped in the front of his shirt followed close behind. I looked back one time to see if Pitt was going to follow, but he was still struggling to get up off the ground out of the slippery mud. We could hear him shouting obscenities at us as we disappeared into the stormy night.

"We ended up spending the night in a shallow cave Billy and I had found years before and had always played in. Billy tore a piece of his shirt off and wrapped the pup's leg up tightly. Billy and the pup were both in pitiful shape.

"We stayed there all the next day talking and thinking out what we were going to do. We decided there was no future for us around Chase any longer, so we would wait until night, break into the mercantile general store and steal some supplies. Then we would go wake up Mack Henry, whose father ran the livery stables. Mack was older than Billy and me, but he was kind of 'slow'. He liked us because we never tormented him like the other kids did. We knew he would fix us up with some horses then we would head out for Texas. We figured we could find work there on some cattle ranch.

"That's what we sure enough did too, and we took that dog with us. Never did give that critter a proper name really, we just called him Dog or Three-foot. His left front leg was gone just below the joint, but that didn't slow him down much, he got around just fine.

"We found a large spread near El Paso that was hard up for ranch hands and they gave us a job. We got room, board and twelve dollars a month pay. There we learned the business of being cowboys... roping, riding, branding and shooting too.

"After about two years of punching cows for a living, Billy got restless and left the dog and me. He took up with a couple of no goods that got him into cattle rustling, robbing banks and stagecoaches.

"In California, Billy and four other fellows tried to rob a wagon loaded with government gold. All of them were shot in the attempt. Billy was the only one to survive his wounds. He was tried and sentenced to five years hard labor in San Quentin prison near San Francisco.

"From prison, Billy wrote quite often to Molly in Chase and to me in Texas. I never was much on writing, but from the letters Billy got from Molly he kept me informed of what was going on in Chase. I thought about Molly often, especially about her having to live with a man like that no good August Pitt. That sweet lady remained faithful to him right up till the day she died. From the stories I heard it certainly wasn't the same with Pitt."

Anger came up into Bud's face again, "W-hy, he ran with every dance hall girl in town I heard. Some said Molly didn't recover from the fever because she just lost the will to go on living the way she was. I reckon she died of a broken heart and spirit.

"Molly missed us terribly, but according to what Billy said in his letters she understood why we had to leave.

"I sent money to Mack Henry to pay for the supplies and the horses we took until I figured I had paid a fair price for everything. Nothing was ever mentioned by anyone, not even after I returned to Chase.

"One day when I came in from about a month out on the range and collected my mail there were three letters from Billy waiting on me. Molly had taken ill the first one said. Molly had gotten worse and wanted Billy and me to come home if possible said the second, and in the third Billy informed me he had been paroled because of her sickness and his good behavior. He was headed for Chase as fast as he could get there and he suggested that I do the same.

"I was sick that I hadn't received the information until then. I packed my gear as quick as I could and left for Chase in a hurry. Three-foot was following close behind.

"The afternoon I arrived, I was too late, Molly's funeral had been that morning. Billy hardly said a word to me until I explained about the letters and why I was late getting there.

"Billy told me Pitt had grumbled through the whole thing saying things like, 'It's just like that old woman to leave me when I needed her most', and, 'she never was much of a cook no-how'.

"While Billy was renewing his friendship with the dog, he told me how much he wished I had shot Pitt that night. I told him that there were times, I wished I had too.

"Billy said, 'I'll tell you Bud, the thought hasn't left my mind'.

"Now, that old dog acted like Billy had never left him. He hung around Billy the rest of the evening, followed him everywhere. It is kind of ironic you know, because that night a storm blew in, much like the one that had come up the night Billy and I left.

"Later on that evening, I left Billy in a saloon that Pitt didn't frequent. I had ridden hard all that day, so I went to bed early in my hotel room.

"Now, the story was told, that about midnight as lightning lit the distant skies, Pitt and two of his so called deputies, came stumbling out of a saloon just across Main Street from the livery stables. They were talking loud, laughing and joking as they staggered along.

"Think about it," the anger flared red hot in Bud's eyes as he spoke. "They had buried the man's wife that very day, and here he was out whooping it up like it was no big deal that the sweetest, dearest persons alive had just died.

"As the wind kicked up and dark clouds rolled in, two figures appeared in the shadows of Main Street. One was a man, the other a dog.

"Pitt and his deputies stopped dead in their tracks when they saw the two shadowy outlines. Pitt demanded, 'Who's that? What ya doin' in the street this time a 'night? Come on out in the light, so's we can see ya'.

"'You remember us, don't you Pitt?' a voice from the shadows answered.

"'I said who are ya? What'd ya want...Us who? Ya mean that...' Pitt stopped in the middle of his sentence when he realized the dog was short one leg.

"'Billy Mason that you? Ya still hangin' around that mangy mutt, are ya?' Pitt's friends chuckled at his little joke.

"'Go ahead and laugh Pitt. You'll be a laughin' out of the other side of yer mouth shortly. Or maybe, at least you'll die with a smile on your face. That's more than we can say for Molly,' the shadowy figure said." Grandpa Bud spoke as if he had those words memorized.

"'What's Molly any yer business? You and that Paxton kid ran off,' said Pitt."

"'It's time you paid your dues, Pitt,' was the reply from the figure in the shadows."

"Pitt's demeanor changed. 'Look here Mason,' he said. 'I'm tard of this. Step aside or we'll go right over ya'. Nothing was heard from the man in the shadows, but a low, deep growl came from the dog.

"'Ah, the heck with ya,' Pitt said. He turned as if to walk away, but instead he jerked his .44, spun around to fire only to catch two .45 slugs in his chest. Pain and astonishment filled Pitt's face as his knees buckled, he fell face down into the street. The dog barked twice. The rain started and a sudden deafening crack of thunder made Pitt's two deputies nearly jump out of their boots as they stood looking down on their dead companion.

"'You boy's clean that garbage off the street and clear out,' the shadowy figure said. 'This town don't need the likes of you hangin' around anymore.' Without argument or hesitation the two deputies did just that. Nothing was heard of them after that night.

"Pitt was dead and that night was the last time anyone in Chase saw Billy Mason until they brought him home in a pine box about ten days later. Billy had tried to hold up a stage and was shot by the shotgun guard.

"Now, ol' Three-foot didn't do much more than lay around on the porch until he died about a year later. I stayed in Chase and became deputy to the new marshal. When he died three years later I took over the job as marshal. Lois Tanner, a local girl became the new school teacher and we got to know each other, fell in love and got married. As for the orphanage, Mom Lois took that over too. Most of the kids were adopted out or grew up and left. A few years later the silver ran out and old Chase started dying. In ninety, I bought the ranch and we moved. Two years later we started the, 'Molly Rhodes Ranch Home for Children'.

"That's the story gal," said Bud, ending it as if there was no more to tell. "No more mystery. We better get back now, don't you think?"

"Yes, I suppose," Julie said as she began rolling the blanket up. "Billy Mason shot August Pitt? How do you know that for sure? Was there an investigation? Did anyone actually see who the shadowy figure was?"

"That's what everyone has always thought," said Bud. "I mean who else could it have been?"

"It could have been you," Julie teased. "You did say you and Billy looked alike didn't you?"

It was obvious that Julie's questioning bothered Grandpa Bud. "I don't know where you're getting these notions, Julie. Everybody in old Chase figured it was Billy Mason and that's good enough for me."

"I'm sorry Grandpa Bud," Julie said. "I didn't mean to upset you. I was just thinking that no one saw who it really was. I mean, it could have been anyone in the town. I am sure a lot of people didn't care for that man. He certainly deserved what he got, I suppose."

"Let's just drop it. I only come up here out of respect for the memory of Miss Molly," Bud said as he hurriedly plucked weeds from around the grave. Then he took off his neckerchief and dusted off the marker.

There was little conversation on the ride back to the lodge. Julie felt bad that she had upset Grandpa Bud. At first she had the suspicion that just maybe he was the one who shot August Pitt, but now, she wasn't sure. "It probably was Billy Mason," she thought, "Grandpa Bud was probably upset over the loss of his friend. After all, they had grown up together just like brothers." Julie cleared her mind, feeling she had no reason to question it anymore.

When they got back to the cabin, Bud told Julie they would leave in the morning. Then he said, "Julie, I want to apologize for being harsh with you earlier. I guess I'm somewhat touchy when it comes to the subject of Miss Molly and Billy. I loved them both and I wish that rotten no-good varmint, August Pitt, had never come into our lives. That's in the past long ago now, and I try not to think about it except once a year."

"I understand Grandpa Bud. No apologies necessary," Julie said. She walked over to him and gave him a hug. She felt her earlier suspicions were surely unfounded. "I love you very much Grandpa Bud," she said, "and, I would never be upset with you for very long no matter what happened." Julie pushed up on her toes and kissed him on the cheek.

A big smile formed on Bud's face and he said, "I love you very much too, gal."

That evening before bed, Bud said as he sat down with his Bible, "You know Julie, Mom Lois and I have been talking a lot lately about what should be done with the ranch after we're gone. I don't know if you have given any thought to it, but we would like to see you come back from college and take over the ranch and the orphanage. You know, teach school there and learn how to run the place. The ranch is going to be yours anyway, but keeping the school going is a different matter. Mom

Lois and me aren't getting any younger you know. Why I'll be sixty-six next month."

"I don't know Grandpa Bud. It is a lot of responsibility. I want to be a teacher, but running the school and the orphanage. I don't know if I could handle all of that."

"Well don't worry yourself about it now. Do think about it though. You've got to get through college first."

"I don't know," Bud said after a brief pause. "Maybe I ought to just sell the ranch and retire. Mom Lois and I don't need all that responsibility in our old age anyway. We would still be leaving you a nice chunk of money and you could do whatever you wanted to with it."

"You do what you think is best for you and Mom Lois," Julie said. "I'm sure the both of you will be around for a long while yet anyway."

After they were packed and ate breakfast the next morning Julie asked, "I'd like to go down to the dock and look at the lake, if I have time?"

"Sure Julie, go ahead. I want to check the car before we leave anyway. Be back within a half-hour or so. Okay?"

"Sure. See you pretty soon."

Julie ran down the hill to the dock. She saw someone fishing off the end. As she approached she saw that it was Mack Henry.

"Hi Mr. Henry, you catching anything?" asked Julie as she ran down the dock.

"Set girl," said Mack Henry. "How I gonna catch any fish with the noise yer makin'."

"O-oh. I am sorry Mr. Henry."

"That okay. I really don't mind that I don't catch no fish. I just like the quiet here in the morning. Set down on the minnow bucket and tell me about yer trip up to Chase. I grew up there you know? Knew your dad when I was young up there too."

"He is my adopted father you know, but I call him Grandpa Bud."

"He was from the orphanage, ya know. I went to school with him and Billy Mason. Nice fella's them two were. I liked'm both. Too bad Billy was a robber though."

"Yes it was, wasn't it," Julie replied.

"Yer grandpa dad tell about Marshal Pitt getting' shot?"

"Yes he did. He told me about the dog and how Billy Mason shot August Pitt in the street that night after Molly's funeral."

"Told ya that same old story, huh?" Mack Henry said with a shy grin. Then he turned back quickly to his fishing.

Julie wrinkled her face and raised an eyebrow. "What do you mean same old story?" Mack ignored her, she asked again, only more insistently. "What do you mean, same old story, Mr. Henry?"

Mack turned and looked at her sheepishly. "You know," he said, "it bein' Billy Mason what done the Marshal in."

"It was Billy. How would you know who it was anyway?" she questioned.

"Cause, I seen and heard the whole thing that night. Watched it from my bedroom window, that how I know. Heck, ol' Billy was gone an hour or more before it happened. I saddled his horse for 'em. Don't worry girl, I ain't told a sole no different, 'cept you and Bud, in all these years. Didn't see where it'd matter. No one cared that ol' Marshal Pitt was dead. He was the meanest man I ever did know.

"I told Bud about seein' him do it after Billy Mason got killed. He asked if I'd told anyone else, I said no. I told him to leave things the way they were. That it might be better that way, he agreed. Nobody cared that Marshal Pitt was gone, and just maybe he deserved to die in the street like a dog. Ha...that funny, like a dog."

Mack expression turned serious, "You won't tell him I told ya, will ya? I should not have a told you, maybe. You can't tell 'em, okay?"

"No. I won't tell," said Julie. "You can trust me to keep a secret."

"Don't think Bud felt good about doin' it though."

"I don't think so either Mr. Henry. I think it bothers him a lot."

"Too bad too. Bud is a nice fella, and so was that Billy Mason. They were my best friends."

"I think so too Mr. Henry. Well, I have to be going. Grandpa Bud wants to get back home. Bye, Mr. Henry. I hope you catch a lot of fish," Julie shouted as she started back up the dock.

"Bye Miss Julie. Ya come back next year."

Julie was the quiet one on the way home this time. She had a lot to think about. When they were about halfway home, Julie looked over at Grandpa

Bud and smiled, he smiled back, his eyes full of kindness and understanding. She wondered how this gentle, caring man could have shot anyone, even a person like August Pitt. She understood why he didn't want anybody to know.

A little while later without thinking she asked, "Grandpa Bud, are you sure that it was Billy Mason who killed August Pitt?"

Bud turned to Julie, eyes narrowed. "I thought we had put that subject to rest, child."

Julie really didn't mean to bring it up again it was just that her curiosity had gotten the best of her. "I'm sorry," she said. "It's just that Mr. Henry...Oh...oh, I mean, never mind."

"What did that old goat tell you anyway? Just when did you see Mack to talk to him. Down at the dock this morning, right?"

"Yes. But, I promised him I wouldn't say anything," Julie said. "Oh why did I ever say anything," she thought. "I'm really sorry Grandpa Bud, I wasn't thinking." Julie's pleading eyes welled up with tears. "Just forget I said anything, okay?"

"He told you about saddling Billy's horse and him leavin' town an hour before Pitt was shot, didn't he?" said Grandpa Bud.

"I promised, I wouldn't say anything," Julie said. A tear rolled down her cheek.

Grandpa Bud pulled the car over to the shoulder of the road and stopped. With kindness and caring in his voice he said, "I'm sorry my dear daughter, don't cry. It's my fault for not telling you the whole story. I thought I wouldn't have to tell it to anyone besides Mom Lois ever again. You see, I didn't care if people thought I shot Pitt, there's been times I wished I had.

"Like I told you before I went to bed early that night. Then, around midnight I was awakened by gun shots down the street. The next thing I knew Billy came galloping down the alley where the window to my room was with ol' Three-foot followin' close behind. I threw up the window as Billy came sliding to a halt and jumped off his horse. He grabbed up Three-foot in his arms and shoved him at me."

"'Here,' he said as he shoved three-foot into my hands. 'Take him. I can't take him with me. It's been nice seein' ya again Bud, but I gotta high-tail-it'."

"'Why, what's goin' on here?' I said."

"'I just put two forty-fives into his useless hide. Pitt's dead in the street'."

"'You did what? You sure he's dead', I said."

"'Damn right he's dead,' said Billy. 'He got his come up'ins for what he did to Molly. Listen Bud, I'd like to stay here an' jaw with ya, but, I think you'll understand if I get ta ridin'. Take care of yerself and stay out'a trouble.' With that, Billy swung up on his horse, and that was the last time I seen him alive.

"Now, there was those in town who, like Mack Henry, thought it was me that night. And really, I didn't care what they thought, so I never said anything one way or another, except to Mom Lois right before I married her.

"Well darling', that's the whole story of what really happened. There's really nothing to fret over. It's all buried and gone now. So, it doesn't really matter anymore except to me."

"I am sorry that I ever doubted you," said Julie. "I really didn't think you could kill anyone, unless you were defending yourself or someone else."

"Can we head for home now, and not mention this again?" asked Grandpa Bud. "I really don't like talking' about it at all."

"Yes, certainly. I won't say anymore on the subject."

Bud pulled the car back out on the road and they headed for home again.

As they drove down the lane that lead to the ranch Julie said, "Grandpa Bud, I've been thinking real seriously about what you said. I think it would be a privilege to follow in Molly's footsteps, as well as yours and Mom Lois'. You know, running and caring for an orphanage, the children and the school. What more could I want as a meaningful career. So, as soon as I get out of college, I will come back and do just that."

"That would be great Julie," Grandpa Bud answered. "But, are you sure that's what you want to do with your life?"

"Yes, I'm sure," said Julie. "I have thought about it thoroughly and that's what I want to do."

"Well, I'm sure you won't be sorry," Grandpa Bud said. "It's a very fulfilling life. Mom Lois and I have no regrets. You're a lovely girl Julie, in more ways than one and I'm proud of you. I know you'll do a fine job and do well for a lot of people."

Julie leaned back in the seat, eyes bright and wide with a smile on her face, content knowing what she was going to do with her life.

THE END

'CHEROKEE KID,' "THOMAS' REVENGE"

I had just come up out of Old Mexico where I had bought a nice string of five mustangs. While riding down a shallow creek bed I came across a rider-less horse and a pack mule drinking from the creek. After taking a good look and finding no one around, I secured my mustangs and picked up the two strays.

"Easy there fella," I said as I gently stroked under the mane of the nervous saddle horse calming him. Ever since I was a boy on the reservation I have had a way with horses. "What's happened to your owner big boy?" I said to the big red sorrel. I ruled out Indians or highwaymen, knowing neither of them would have left the animals behind. I decided I would take them along, maybe I would run across the owner hurt or something worse on the trail.

Down a ways, the creek took a sharp bend around a high rimmed ridge. As I approached I heard an echo of voices and laughter coming from around the bend, so I held up. I figured I had better take a look at what I might be riding into before I made the corner. I tied off the string back a ways, which now numbered seven, and found the easiest way to top the ridge where I could see what was going on down below.

Once on top of the rim I positioned myself so I would not be seen as I took a look below. On a long sandbar down below were four men. Two were setting on a log size piece of driftwood sharing a bottle of mescal. One of the men on the log was a big burly fellow with a beard I recognized as

Russian Bill, I didn't know the other man. A man with long, straight black hair and dressed somewhat Apache style I recognized as a half-breed renegade nicknamed, The Indian. He was sharpening a large hunting knife on a stone. The last man, a young blonde haired fellow, was staked out with his feet tied high to another piece of driftwood. He was stripped to just a pair of faded red flannels and he looked a bit roughed up.

The Indian finished sharpening his knife, tested the edge and went over to a large fire that had burned down to just coals. He kicked the coals and spread them out across an area about five or six feet long. Knowing what The Indian had in mind I went to my saddle scabbard and drew out my Sharps. I rested it through a fork in a nearby Palo Verde and took careful aim. (A buffalo hunter had willed me the rifle just before he died after I had given him a drink of water. I had found the poor soul lying on a hillside with a half dozen arrows stuck in him.)

The Sharps had an extended barrel and a precision long-range sight. I could pick a needle off a barrel cactus at a hundred yards with the Sharps.

I thumbed back the hammer and squeezed off a shot that sent the hunting knife flying from The Indian's hand. Quickly I ejected the spent shell and slipped in another cartridge and shattered the whiskey bottle in Russian Bill's hand as he stood up.

I shouted down as I reloaded, "The next one, somebody dies unless you clear out." With that I took off the last fellow's hat. The trio was on their horses riding hell-bent in short order after that. I waited a spell before I left my position. I wanted to make sure those three would not decide to return. So, when they were a quarter mile or so downstream I took aim and sent one buzzing over their heads. I didn't know about the one fellow, but Russian Bill and The Indian were a couple of the meanest scum around and they didn't scare easily.

I went back, collected the string, and led them around to the sandbar where the young man was tied down. I swung my leg over and slid off my horse. As I walked toward the young man on the ground I reached behind my neck and pulled my Arkansas Toothpick out of its sheath. As I approached, knife in hand, the young man's light blue eyes got as big as dishpans. I cut the ropes off his feet and hands.

"Hey mister," said the young man, "that's my horse and pack mule you got there."

"Kind of figured that," I said. "You know, you could have thanked me for saving your hide instead of accusing me of being a horse thief."

"How do I know you ain't with those fellas that jest left off outa here," said the young fellow.

"Maybe I should have let The Indian make a fire-walker out of you. Then you would have been real appreciative that I came along when I did."

"What ya mean fire-walker?"

I pointed to the coals with my knife and said, "I mean that The Indian with the hunting knife was getting ready to slice off a couple layers of the soles of your feet. Then he was going to make you walk through the hot coals he had spread out over there."

"Heck, I wouldn't have walked through those coals," he said.

"Let me tell you something son," I said. "Assuredly, The Indian knows ways to persuade you to do what he wants. And there are not any of them pleasant."

"Well," the young fellow paused, then said thoughtfully, "Mebee yer right. I reckon I otta thank ya fer comin' along when you did. Thanks mister." He extended a hand, "Al'm Thomas Henderson."

I put my knife in my other hand, grabbed the young man's hand and shook it firmly. I said, "My given name is Lee Henry Forest, but everybody that knows me calls me, Cherokee."

The young man raised a questioning brow and said, "Cherokee? I heard of you. Yer the Cherokee Kid?"

"Well, some have called me that. But, I'm getting a bit too old for that Kid business."

"Yeah, yer a bounty hunter and you hunt and kill men for money," said Thomas.

"Sure," I said firmly. "I do not consider myself a bounty hunter though. I have brought in a few wanted men that I have run across on the trail and collected some reward money. However, I have never killed a man unless he was intending harm to me or someone else." I slipped my knife into place back over my shoulder.

Blue eyes flashing with excitement Thomas said, "Yeah, well I heard you brought in Bob Lape 'cross a saddle."

"Sure I did," I said. "He and his partner made the mistake of trying to rob me out on the road."

"Bob Lape was s'posed to be a fierce man," Thomas said.

"Maybe so, but he should not have tried to take what was mine.

"Enough about me." I walked over and pulled a canteen off my saddle. "What were you doing in the company of the likes of Russian Bill and The Indian?" I unstopped the canteen and offered it to Thomas.

He took a big gulp from the canteen, swished it around in his mouth and then swallowed it. "OW… oh," Thomas winced as he touched his finger to a cut on his lip. "Well," Thomas said, "five months ago on our farm back in Texas I was out plowin' the fields with that there mule." He nodded toward the pack mule and the horse I had found. "Those three fellers you ran off come up on me. They started pokin' fun at me and laughin' 'mongst themselves. They commenced to callin' me filthy names, sayin' how they had no use for sodbusters. The big one rode into me with his horse and almost knocked me down. The mule spooked, broke loose from the plow and ran off. The other two fellers rode round behind me. That's when I was struck with somethin' hard from behind and I went out.

"I come round presently with my face in the fresh plowed ground and blood runnin' in my eyes from where I was hit from behind. I looked up and saw heavy smoke in the direction of our farmhouse. My head was just a bustin' so bad that tears ran down my face. I had trouble seein', but I got up and run t'ward the house with all I could muster. When I got there, our house was ablaze nearly gone, and I found my ma makin' over my pa who was layin' on the ground bleedin' from the head. Stephanie, that's my little sister, she's eleven, was sobbin' somethin' awful. I noticed my ma's clothes were torn an' half off. Her face was bruised up and red, with blood comin' out of her nose. She had a shameful look about her.

"'O-Oh, Thomas,' my ma sobbed, 'They've killed yer father.'" Thomas' eyes dropped and he looked down. "That's when I realized… he wasn't breathin'.

"Stephanie ran over and grabbed me tight. Cryin' terrible she told me, 'they did dreadful things to mommy, Thomas'." Glassy eyed hatred that could punch a hole in a man welled up in Thomas' eyes, and through his teeth he said, "She didn't need to tell no more, I knew what they had done.

"I made arrangements for my ma and sister to stay with friends," said Thomas. "Then after I sold our hogs and milk cow for travelin' money, I took out after those three devils." Eyes filled with fiery hatred, Thomas said, "I promise ya I'm gonna kill those three fellers fer what they did. I won't rest, nor give up, till they're all dead."

"Mighty powerful talk," I said, "for a young man I just saved from being tortured by the very men he is going to kill."

I went over to a pile of clothes I knew had to be Thomas' I picked them up and underneath the pile was an old Walker Colt. "You going to kill those men with this are you Thomas?" I said as I picked up the heavy pistol.

"It shoots, and it'll shore 'nough kill," said Thomas.

"I will not argue that," I said. "But, if you are going to deal with the kind of men you are going after, you had better have something you can handle with lightening quick accuracy."

Thomas was still sitting on the ground as I dumped his clothes in his lap and quick drew my Remington cartridge conversion. I spun it three or four times and worked the hammer and then planted it firmly back in place.

"Well," said Thomas, "I whoosh I could handle a hand gun like that. But, I don't happen to have one to practice with, so I'll just make do." I went to my saddlebags and found a Colt .45 Army I had for a spare. After buying it I found I still favored the Remington changeover. "Here," I said as I tossed it to Thomas. "Try this and see if it suits you."

Thomas caught it. "I can't take this," he said, "Too much money for a farm boy."

"I didn't say I was selling it to you. I said see how it suits you. If you like it, I might just lone it to you for a while."

Thomas carefully worked it and inspected it admiringly. "Shore I like it," he said.

I nodded up toward the ridge I had shot down from. "I'll tell you what Thomas," I said, "I am going back up on that ridge and make camp for the night. You're welcome to join me for the night if you have a mind. You had better dress yourself first though."

"I wanna get after those fellers right away," Thomas insisted.

"I can understand that, but you won't do any good in the dark. You can get an early start in the morning. Those three won't be riding in the dark either, so come on along and get some rest."

"I s'pose maybe yer right," said Thomas. "All right then, I'll camp for the night, but I mean to get an early start."

"I think that is what I said."

Thomas put his clothes on and we rode up to the ridge and made camp. I doctored Thomas' minor wounds with some herbs and then he done the cooking. He cooked up some fatback and beans along with some corndodgers. He had coffee too; I had run out and hadn't had any for four or five days, it was a welcome indulgence. The fatback and beans were welcomed too, seeing how I had been living on bacon, hardtack and biscuits for some time.

After the meal I pulled a flask of Canadian whiskey out of my saddlebags. I poured a shot into Thomas' coffee and about twice that much into my own. "It will take the edge off and help you sleep good," I said.

"All right," said Thomas. "I ain't had much rest since I left home." He took a hardy sip and made an ugly face as he swallowed. "Not b-bad," he said as he choked a bit. I could tell he had little experience with whiskey, because the Canadian was a mellow blend and went down smooth as silk.

The moon was near full and bright that night; it lit things up almost like it was day. Coyotes yelped and carried on in the distance, an owl hooted as a mild breeze brightened the embers of the fire. I wrote in my journal that I keep as I sipped the coffee-whiskey mix. Thomas poked the fire with a stick. Suddenly he said, "Say, can I ask you a personal question? I mean, I don't wanna be too nosey, but I'm curious about somethin'."

"I wouldn't want you to go through life curious about me," I said. "Ask away, I'll see if I can give you a respectable answer."

"They call you The Cherokee Kid. Now, don't take no offense, I mean, I see you wear your hair long and yer wearin' those moccasin boots an' all. But you don't look like you got no Injun blood in you."

"No offense taken. I do have Indian blood in my background though," I said. "My grandmother was a full blooded Cherokee, which made my mother half Cherokee. My grandfather was a white man known as The Swede. He was a mountain man who lived and hunted with the Cherokee people for many years before he died. My father was an Indian agent, so when he married my mother and she had me, I grew up on the reservation amongst the Cherokee people back in Indian Territory. I lived with and learned from the Cherokee until I struck out on my own. I am rather proud of my Cherokee blood, which is why I have never objected to being called the Cherokee Kid. Like I said earlier, I am getting a bit old for the Kid part of that title.

"You know Thomas," I said, "you never did tell me how you got into that predicament down there on the sandbar."

"Oh, that," said Thomas. "I ain't too awfully proud of lettin' them varmints get the drop on me like that.

"You see," said Thomas, "I found out by askin' around in El Paso that those men were headin' for Tombstone. So I picked up their trail while back and was followin' it down the creek bed. When I made the bend in the river, that Injun feller jumped down from a ledge and knocked me off my horse. My horse and the mule ran off as we scuffled in the water. The other two joined in and wrestled me to the ground. Then they made me strip down to my flannels.

"The Injun told me he was gonna fix it so's I wouldn't be so anxious to follow them anymore. That's when he hog-tied me and started the fire."

"It's a doggoned good thing I came along when I did. They would have crippled you for life, if you had survived that is. I don't know Thomas, maybe you had better give this up. Those men you are after are some of the meanest, toughest scum I know of. You are just not experienced enough to deal with the likes of them."

Thomas jumped to his feet. "I'll tell you," he said as he pointed his finger at me from across the fire, "those men are gonna pay for what they did and I'll not rest 'til thar all dead. I won't make the same mistake twice and let them get the drop on me again."

"Well then," I said, "if you feel that strong about it I had better show you how to handle that .45 I loaned you."

"I'd be much obliged if you would," said Thomas. "In fact, I got a hundred and fifty dollars in my pack that I'd be willing to give you if you'd ride with me 'til I put those fellers in the dirt."

"I don't know Thomas," I said as I scratched my chin. "I suppose I could get a fair price for my ponies in Tombstone. Yes, I reckon I would ride that far with you anyway. That would give me a few days to teach you some finer points of being a pistoleer. I would feel pretty bad loaning it to you and you not knowing how to handle it proper. I'll sleep on it," I said. "I am going to get some shuteye now." I pulled my hat down on my face, leaned back on my saddle and then pulled my Indian blanket up over my shoulders. "I suggest you do the same, Thomas."

Pistol shots at the crack of dawn abruptly awakened me the next morning. I had my .44 cocked and aimed before I realized it was Thomas practicing with the Colt I had given him. All I could see was his silhouette in a cloud of smoke against a golden morning sky.

"Doggone Thomas, I darn near shot you," I said.

"Good. Yer awake," said Thomas. "Ya got anymore cartridges for this here shootin' ir'n."

"How could I be anything but awake," I said. "Yeah, I have got more cartridges for it, but I am not going to get them before I have some of your coffee."

After a short breakfast I got a box of .45 cartridges out of my saddlebags, walked over to

Thomas who was sitting impatiently by the campfire. I said, "Give me that Colt, Thomas."

"What fer? I can load it my own self," said Thomas.

"Maybe so," I said. "But, if this morning was an example of how you can handle a six-gun, then you had better let me show you a few things."

"What do ya mean?" said Thomas. He held up the Colt. "I can handle this here shootin' ir'n just fine."

I snatched the Colt from Thomas' hand. "Look here youngster," I said, "I don't mean to be harsh, but if you think you can go up against the sort of men you are dealing with here and not be an efficient gunfighter, you are sorely mistaken and you are going to end up very dead in short order. I am not taking responsibility for that.

"Now," I said, "I'll show you a few things to work on and then you can practice. I do not want you wasting those cartridges like you were doing earlier. For one thing, they cost a pretty penny and for another, you have to make every shot count."

"All right Cherokee, I'll listen to you," Thomas said humbly. "I know you got experience bringin' in desperadoes and I'll abide by yer instructions. So, let's get this started."

"All right then," I said as I thumbed six cartridges into the chambers. "When you are shooting it out with some hombre, there are times when you cannot take careful aim like you were doing. And you sure cannot flinch and blink every time the gun fires neither. You have to learn to shoot from the hip at close range. It is a matter of being able to point right at what you are trying to hit. Since you don't have a gun belt at this time you should stick the pistol in the front of your pants like this." I demonstrated. "Then, you draw the pistol out to your hip, like this, and fan off a few."

I fan fired two quick shots that took small limbs off the Palo Verde tree I had rested my Sharps in the day before.

"W-OW," said Thomas. "Did you intend to knock those two limbs off when you shot?"

I ignored his question and said, "Now stand up here and give it a try." I handed the Colt to Thomas.

"No, not the Polo Verde," I said. "You just try and hit that scrub oak over there." It was a lot closer than the Polo Verde.

Thomas tried to copy my movements but was awkward. His first shot went wild off into the distance, yards beyond the tree. The second shot hit its mark only a bit too high.

"Not too bad for your first try," I said. "What you need to do is slow down some, point right at your target. And listen, we are not trying to be sharp shooters here; don't try to hit the fella between the eyes, point between his shoulders and his belt line. You want to stop him in his tracks, and that .45 will do just that. With a steady hand fan off a couple of shots and it will be even more effective."

Thomas practiced what I had showed him and got fairly efficient at it. Before we started packing up to leave I said, "Thomas, I want to explain to you that shooting a tree and shooting a man are two entirely different things indeed. For one thing a man will shoot back, even after he is hit and dying. He could kill you on his way out. That is why it is important to make your first shot count and that there is no hesitation when you take it. You have got to make it your resolve before you face a man that it is him or you."

Thomas nodded without saying a word. The look in his eyes said he had every intention of taking down all three of the men that had caused him such grief.

Every time we stopped along the way to Tombstone, Thomas practiced his draw and shoot. He caught on fast, but I wasn't sure how he would do if he had to face a man and do the same thing. We were short on conversation throughout our trek, which suited me just fine. I am not much for small talk anyway.

We had been in Arizona Territory for a short time when Thomas was put to the test. The trail was leading us through an arroyo when three riders appeared in front of us from out of almost nowhere. At first I thought it might be Russian Bill and the others, but as they came closer I saw that it was not. Even at a distance I knew from their manner they were more than likely highwaymen and up to no good.

When the men were close enough for me to size them up, I said, "Thomas, when I say, Do it, you take out the man on the left. I will take the other two."

"You mean…shoot 'em?" said Thomas.

"Yes sir, I mean just that," I answered. "Those three are up to no good. And, I am sure they mean to cause us harm. Trust me youngster, there is going to be trouble. So, prepare yourself for a confrontation."

As the three drew near I saw that the leader was a Mexican wearing a thick brimmed sombrero. The one to the left that I had told Thomas to take care of was of Mexican descent also. He carried a Winchester laid across the front of his saddle and he had a full cartridge belt across his chest from over his shoulder. The other fellow was a white man, a dude, probably a saloon gambler from the looks of him. His long black coat was pulled back to expose a nickel-plated six-gun that he wore in cross draw fashion for quick draw from a sitting position.

It was pretty obvious that the three had no intention of letting us pass by. They would adjust their position on the trail anytime we made an attempt to adjust ours.

"Hold up," I told Thomas, "Let them come to us." We stopped and waited for the trio to come ahead. The three stopped short of us about eight feet across our path. There was no doubt that the Mexican in the sombrero was the leader. He eyed my mustangs and Thomas' pack mule intently.

"Nice ponies, señor," he said in a thick gravel voice with a heavy Mexican accent. "My friends and I would like to have them." He glanced over his shoulder at his companions. "What do you think amigos?" They gave him dastardly smile in reply.

"I'm taking them to Tombstone to sell," I said. "But, if I can get my price, I would be willing to part with them now."

The Mexican leader chuckled. "Oh-ho-ho, no

señor," he said. Once again he glanced over his shoulder at his companions. Then he leaned forward in the saddle and locked eyes with me in an icy dark glare. His almost black and bloodshot eyes danced as he spoke slowly and intently. "We had no intentions of buying them my friend. We thought you would give them to us in a gesture of good will between our two countries." That brought a sinister smile to the faces of him and his companions.

"Your thinking isn't too awfully good on that then," I said. "I am not giving these horses up to nobody...especially, not to the likes of you three hombres."

I knew the leader would make his move now, so I shouted, "DO IT THOMAS," and went for my Remington. Before he could clear leather I took the leader right out of the saddle with a shot to his chest. He went tumbling backward as his horse reared. Quick as lightening I blasted the gambler and he went much the same way. Then, I felt the impact and sting of a bullet hitting and passing through my left forearm as I held my reins up to control my horse.

Like I had feared Thomas had hesitated before doing what I had told him. This gave the man with the rifle time enough to get off a shot. Thomas did shoot all right, and he did hit his mark fatally, but it cost me an arm wound.

The string was excited and jerking at their leads. So I dismounted and calmed them as best I could with one hand. Thomas had dismounted too, but he was in a nearby bush losing his breakfast.

The bullet had passed through the meaty part of my forearm. Fortunately there were no broken bones, but it felt like one might have been chipped. It was a clean wound and I knew if I cleaned it up properly and dressed it with some Indian potions I had it would heal presently though being a might sore and stiff for a while.

I was washing my arm with my bandana and some water from the water skin on the mule when Thomas came over to me and said, "I'm terrible sorry Cherokee. I know I got you shot. I just ain't never killed a man before."

"Well, I understand," I said. "I'm not too happy about it, but I understand. I will tell you Thomas, fate allowed you one mistake, but I wouldn't count on another. You hesitate in a situation like that and you will end up dead before you know it. I don't mean to shake you, but that's the fact. And if you aren't going to play by those rules, you had just better head on back to that farm in Texas and take care of your mother and your sister right now."

"I'm goin' back to the farm all right, right after I kill those three no-goods for what they done."

"Well then, let's tie those three to their saddles and we will take them into Tombstone and see if they're wanted for anything."

When we arrived in Tombstone I went directly to the County Sheriff's Office and gave the Sheriff my story about the three hold-up men. He looked them over and as I suspected, two of them had bounties on their heads. I collected three hundred dollars and a thank you from the county, which I split with Thomas. He was reluctant to take the money at first saying he should not get paid for killing someone and besides that he figured I was the one that did all the work. I convinced him it wasn't wrong to protect yourself and rid the world of such vermin at the same time. I also told him he would need the money to get back home, so he saw my point and accepted the money.

I also found out from the Sheriff about Russian Bill and his bunch. To Thomas' disappointment Russian Bill had tried to molest a barkeeper's wife and the barkeep had to shoot him dead with a double barrel shot gun in self-defense. Thomas was a bit upset when he received that information, but what could he do, someone had saved him the trouble of confronting him.

After a query around town we found out that The Indian and the other fellow, who was a dying old drunk named Manny Fletch, went up to Charleston to find work at the mill. So, after peddling my ponies to a local rancher for a good price and spending an uneventful night in an interesting town we headed up Charleston way to flush out the two.

In Charleston we learned that the two were living in an old miners shack just a few miles outside of town. I wanted to go on out and take care of business. Thomas objected however, it was Sunday and he did not think it proper to do any killing on the Lord's Day as he put it. I did not want to argue that point so we waited.

Early next morning found us behind a hill looking down on a rundown adobe cabin about fifty yards away. Thomas and I were making out our plan of attack when a voice from behind ordered, "Turn slowly with those hands held high."

We complied with the instructions and when we were turned we faced the cold heartless eyes of The Indian. "Ease those pistols out and drop them to the ground," he said. Seeing how he had a rifle trained on me we again complied.

"What is your business here?" he said. Before we could answer his eyes narrowed and he tightened his brow curiously, "I know you," he said. "You're that dumb kid who followed us on the trail here while back. And...and, I know you too. Cherokee, ain't it?"

"That's what they call me," I said.

"We-ll, what am I gonna do with you two? You fellas march on down to the cabin there and let's figure on what I'm going to do with you." As we headed down toward the cabin The Indian laughed saying, "This might just be fun. I guess you didn't learn anything that day at the river a while back, did you, boy? And, the one shootin' at us...that must have been you, huh, Cherokee?"

"HEY Manny, open up in there," said The Indian as we approached the door. "I got something out here you will want to see."

"Ya geet us a pheasant did ya?" said the voice from inside. Manny unbolted and opened the heavy wood door. "Who'a these fellas?" said Manny as he squinted trying to recognize us. The Indian prodded us through the door with the rifle.

"Get on over there to the table and sit," The Indian said. "You remember this kid don't you Manny. He's the one I was going to skin here awhile back."

"Oh…yeah…yeah, I member now," Manny said. "But, what he doin' here? And, who da udder feller?"

"Good question," said The Indian with a mean glance our way. "What's your business here, Cherokee?"

"I come to kill the both of ya," Thomas threatened.

Manny's eyes grew wide and fearful. "What fer ya wanna kill us fer?"

"For what you all done to my family back in Texas." Thomas was full of rage. "I'll see you both dead if it takes my dyin' breath." Thomas sprang up from his seat and it got him a rifle butt to the side of his head. He went sprawling across the floor.

"Gutsy little pup, huh?" said The Indian.

It was time for me to make my move. I backhanded Manny who was to my left and this sent him back against the wall with a hard thud. I went for my long knife behind my neck, which The Indian fortunately had not noticed under my shirt. I threw it hard and true from over my shoulder and it sank deep into The Indian's chest who had turned to face me. He buckled immediately and fell to the floor motionless.

Thomas, on his hands and knees, crawled quickly across the floor to The Indian's lifeless body and pulled a .44 out of his belt. Thomas, though groggy, struggled to his feet and walked over to Manny who was sitting against the wall coughing uncontrollably. Thomas thumbed back the hammer of the .44 and pointed it directly at Manny's head. "Now it's yer turn to die, just like my pa."

Thomas stood frozen in place aiming at Manny's head. Manny got his cough under control presently, he looked up into Thomas' light blue eyes and said, "Go head kid, kill me. But, mey I say somp'n firse?"

"Go right ahead. It's prob'ly more'n you gave my pa, but go ahead."

"I weren't fer what my pards did ta yer folks," Manny said. "I told 'em it weren't right. I told 'em they'd pay som' day, and they did. Al'm plumb shamed thet I stood by and dent do nuttin' whilst they did thet god-awful thing. Al'm a dyin' man any how's, and I don't think ya ought ta make yerself a killer by shootin' the likes of me. I mean you'd be doin' me a favor if'n ya ended it here and now. But, ya look like a decent young feller and ya shouldn't mess up yer life by killin' me."

"Nice speech mister," said Thomas. "But that don't make for no forgiveness."

"I hain't askin' fer no fergiveness. Jess think about whet yer doin' here."

"Be good if you listened to him Thomas," I said. "He is making good sense."

Thomas looked over at me, a sorrowful tear rolled down his cheek. "Yer right mister," he said, "I ain't no killer." Thomas tossed the .44 to me and I caught it. Thomas had decided to leave Manny with his conscience for whatever time he had left to live.

It has been six months or so since Thomas and I parted company. He went back to Texas and started farming again. Getting along pretty well I gathered from the letter he sent to me at my address in Fort Bowie. He sent a picture of him and his sister and mother, a fine looking family. He also sent along a picture of a sweet young lady that he said he was seeing regular. He thanked me for my help and the money I had given him. He had returned my Colt before we parted, said he did not think he would ever need it again, that he would find another way of settling matters. You know, he probably will, but as for me and the road I travel, it just is not practical. I think Thomas will do just fine though.

》   《

THE SAMARITAN

"Grandpa, tell us a story about the good old days. Grandma will send us to bed in just a little while."

"Yeah, tom on Dranpa, tell us a tory about dood o days."

"Please Grandfather we want to hear a story. May I sit on your lap?"

"Yeah me too Dranpa."

"All right kids. I reckon I can recollect a story that I haven't told you yet. Now Randy, you sit here on the arm of the chair and lean back on my shoulder."

"Oh tay, Dranpa. Help me up, peas.

"There... There you go little one."

"Now, Beth you sit on my knee and lean on the other shoulder. Tim you can sit there on the floor and lean against my leg. How's that everyone?"

"Sure Grandpa. But, hurry and get started before Grandma comes and sends us to bed."

"All right children, here we go-

You see there was this young fella, who was a farmer from Kansas, traveling through South Texas, just this side of New Mexico. He had sold his parent's farm, which he had inherited, and was headed out, to California. There, he planned to buy some land, build a home, plant a vineyard and then find himself a sweet young lady and get married. Trouble was, just outside of a little town called Resolution, a trio of rowdy cowhands, who hated farmers or sodbusters as they called them, caught up with him. The three beat the poor fellow severely, ran off his team of horses and rifled through his belongings. Then they left him for dead with his wagon alongside the road.

He was near death, moaning something terrible when, Mr. Pullman, the bank president, came by on his way into town. When he saw the farm wagon and the pitiful stranger lying at the side of the road he guided his carriage to the opposite side and went on, paying the hurt man no mind at all. You see, the town of Resolution was a small cattle ranching community and no one around there cared a hoot for sod busting squatters.

Well, not long after Mr. Pullman passed by, another so-called, fine upstanding citizen of Resolution came by on his way into town to do some business. This was Parker James, a well-to-do rancher and business leader in and around Resolution. Everyone respected his authority and knew him as P.J.

"Like my pajamas Dranpa."

"Well sort of, but that was what people called him."

When P.J. saw the wagon and farming equipment scattered around, he knew immediately that it belonged to a settler. So, he also ignored the pitiable figure lying beside the road and steered his buckboard wide around the scene.

Now, the next person to come along was a lean young trail drover by the name of Johnny Lee Samaritan. He had saved up some money and was also headed for California. His plan, however, was to do some prospecting, hoping to strike it rich.

When Johnny Lee, as he was known, came upon this unfortunate sight, he jumped from his horse and ran to the man's aid. He stripped his neckerchief from around his neck and wet it with water from his canteen and cleaned the man's wounds as best he could. Then he put the fellow under the wagon, out of the sun and followed the tracks left by the team of horses. He found them not far away drinking at a small pond. After hitching up the team and tying his horse at the rear of the wagon, Johnny Lee headed toward town. About three-quarters of a mile outside of Resolution, Johnny Lee pulled up at a Way Station and carried the injured farmer in his arms inside.

A round Mexican woman was cooking at a brick hearth and a heavy, unshaven innkeeper met him as soon as he came in the door. "What's this?" said the innkeeper.

"This man's hurt bad and needs help. You got a bed where I can put him down?" Johnny Lee said.

"We-ll, yeah, but, who's this fella and why'd ya bring him here?"

"I don't know who he is. All I know is I found him on the road by his wagon, near dead. Now, where's that bed?"

"In there," the innkeeper said pointing toward a door in the back. "But, I usually get two bits a day for the room."

"I'll pay you whatever's necessary," Johnny Lee said. Then he impatiently brushed by the innkeeper and headed toward the room. After making the man as comfortable as possible Johnny

Lee, came back in to ask the innkeeper about finding a doctor to tend for the injured man.

"There's a Doc in Resolution, I think," the innkeeper said. "Don't have much faith in 'em myself though, heard he's just a drunk anyways."

"No matter, that man needs attention. You watch over him 'til I get back, and see to it he gets water or whatever he needs. Don't worry I'll cover any cost involved." Johnny Lee put his hand to the Colt on his hip. "And mister, don't let him die while I'm gone; I'd take it real personal if I came back here with the doctor and he was dead. You get my drift, innkeeper?"

"Shore, I'll see to it he's cared for. You just hurry with that doctor then."

"All right then, I'm heading for town. You feed and water his team while I'm gone too."

The innkeeper frowned; he didn't like doing much of anything, so he just shook his head.

In Resolution Johnny Lee found the Doctors Office, but no one was there. Remembering what the innkeeper had said about the Doctor being a drunk he headed for the only saloon in town.

Johnny Lee looked up at the weather worn, washed out storefront sign over the entrance of the saloon, it read: BIG DAN'S WHITE FRONT SALOON. He pushed through the doors and looked around through squinted eyes trying to adjust to the dimly lit room. There was a rotund giant of a man with a full beard behind the bar, Big Dan no doubt. Three cowboys leaned on the bar talking and they took instant notice of the stranger and became silent when he came in. A middle-aged fellow in a wrinkled black suite was sitting at a table by himself. A bottle of cheap whiskey and a half-full glass sat in front of him. Johnny Lee took this to be the Doctor and went over to where he sat.

"You the Doctor in these here parts?" said Johnny Lee.

"That is what has kept me around here and in whiskey for the last eight years," the man said.

"I got a man badly beaten out at the Way Station. He needs the attention of a Doctor right away."

"I will go to my office and get my medical bag," said the Doctor. Then he threw down his whiskey and said, "You go down to the livery and have my carriage readied."

"Sure thing Doc," said Johnny Lee.

As the Doctor and Johnny Lee were leaving, the roughest looking of the three cowboys stepped in front of their path and put a restraining hand on Johnny Lee's chest. "This fella you found on the road a plow-chaser, sonny?"

"I suppose he might be," Johnny Lee said.

"We're cattle men around here, sonny. An' we don't take kindly to sod-busters, or strangers neither for that matter."

"Well, I'll tell you mister, I've herded a few cows myself and I'll help any man that's hurt and needs attention. And, I don't take kindly to being called sonny, or to pushy cowpunchers putting their hands on me. I ain't looking for no trouble, but there's sure enough gonna be some if you don't take your hand off of me right now."

Deadly silence filled the saloon and cold, dark hateful eyes stared right into Johnny Lee's. Then Parker James' voice from the doorway broke the eerie quiet. "Let it go for now Frank." There was no response, just the evil stare into Johnny Lee's eyes. Johnny Lee stood his ground without a blink or a flinch. "Let it go for now, Frank!" said Parker James a second time.

The Doctor pushed his way between the two men, thus breaking the concentration and said, "You two can kill one another some other time, I got an injured man to attend to."

Frank's manner abated and he said to the Doctor, "You best not be attending to no plow-chasers if you know what's good for ya, Doc."

"I have never let you tell me who I can tend to, and I am sure the hell not going to start today, Frank," said the Doctor without even so much as turning around.

"Well, I suppose this fellow will be all right in a few days," said the Doctor after checking the man over and treating his injuries. "It's a darn good thing you came along when you did, though. If he would have been left out there to the elements any longer there is a good chance he would have died in just a few hours."

"All right Doc, thanks. How much do I owe you for coming out here?" said Johnny Lee.

"I tell you young man, seeing you stand up to Frank Coker is enough payment for me. I never liked that man from the first time I laid eyes on him. He is a bad one that is for sure."

"Listen Doc, I got to give you something for your troubles."

"All right, if you insist," the Doctor said. "Then get ol' Solace there to pour me about three-fingers of that, good whiskey, he keeps hid away for himself."

Johnny Lee convinced the innkeeper to set up the bottle and two glasses of his good whiskey, but only after offering him a premium price. Then the three, Johnny Lee, the innkeeper and the Doctor sat sipping the whiskey while the Mexican woman, the innkeeper's wife, fixed them some tortilla's and beans. Since it was late in the evening the Doctor spent the night, as did Johnny Lee. Johnny Lee paid for everything, since the innkeeper was unwilling to let anything go free gratis.

Next morning the Doctor and Johnny Lee went in to check on the patient. He was making a good recovery and sat up in bed. He told them his name was Roderick Travelier, and that he had been on his way to California from Kansas when three men attacked him. From his description it was obvious the men were, Frank Coker and the other two cowboys who were at Big Dan's White Front Saloon the day before. Roderick paused in the middle of a sentence, wrinkled his brow, and said, "Did anyone find a small tin box with a brass lock on it?"

"Yes, I found the box," said Johnny Lee. "But, there was no lock on it, or anything in it.

"Oh-h no-o," Roderick said. "That was my life savings, all I had. There was three-thousand dollars in that box."

"Don't worry Roderick," said Johnny Lee, "We'll see what we can do about getting your money back. I'll contact the County Sheriff and get him to help." The Doctor gave Roderick some medicine to calm him down and he and Johnny Lee went out of the room to let him rest.

Johnny Lee and the Doctor sat drinking coffee talking over the matter. "I don't know whether it will do any good to contact the County Sheriff or not," said the Doctor. "I think ol' P.J.'s probably got him on his payroll too."

"We-ll, I'm gonna look..." Johnny Lee was interrupted by the sound of riders coming up outside. He looked through the window; it was Parker James, in his buckboard, Frank Coker and the two other cowboys on horseback. Johnny Lee got up and hurried to his gear and pulled out his Winchester, checked the load and headed for the front door.

Solace, the innkeeper stopped Johnny Lee at the door. "I don't want no trouble with that bunch out there," he said, "P.J. owns this territory and I don't want no trouble with him. That Frank Coker is a man killer for shore, I tell ya."

Johnny Lee ignored the warning and pushed by the innkeeper and walked out on the porch.

The four held up in the middle of the Way Station's lot. Everyone stayed where they were except for Frank Coker. He dismounted and walked to the end of the reins of his horse and dropped them. He then stopped and stood his ground, stone-faced and evil looking about five steps ahead of his horse.

"I see that squatter's wagon is still here," said Parker James. "All of you are gonna have to move on, right now, or there's gonna be some serious trouble."

Keeping his eyes trained on Frank Coker, Johnny Lee said, "We'll be movin' on as soon as Mr. Travelier is able, and I get back his three-thousand dollars your men stole from him."

Adjusting himself in the buckboard seat, Parker James said, "What's he talking about... three-thousand dollars?"

With guilty eyes the two mounted cowboys looked toward Frank Coker and shrugged their shoulders sheepishly. Without a blink or taking his cold heartless eyes off of Johnny Lee, Frank Coker said, "Who knows what this pups talkin' about P.J. I'd say he's probably been out in the sun too long. Besides, there ain't no sod bustin' plow-chaser got that kind of money no-ways. And, if he did have it, maybe you're the one took it."

With a distinct metallic action, Johnny Lee levered his Winchester into readiness. "Look here you boys," Johnny Lee said, "I know you all got that money and I aim to get it back. And, I aim to get it back right now."

"If you fellas got that money," said Parker James, "Give it up. I ain't payin' ya to rob people, just to keep them settlers movin' on."

"We ain't got no damned money," said Frank Coker. "Ya know sonny," Frank said with hell in his eyes, "I've had enough of yer lip." Frank's hand dropped to the .44 at his side. Before he cleared leather, Johnny Lee answered with the Winchester. A bullet pierced through Frank Coker's forearm, just four or five inches above his wrist, and the .44 went flying from his hand into the dust. Frank dropped to one knee clutching his arm tightly, gnashing his teeth and wincing in pain.

In an instant Johnny Lee levered another cartridge into place and covered the other men with his Winchester, pausing briefly on each one. Parker James said, "You men...if you got that fella's money give it to him. I don't need that kind of trouble."

One of the mounted cowboys spoke up. "It's in Coker's saddle bags in his poke. We ain't spent nary a cent of it yet."

Johnny Lee trained his rifle on the cowboy and said, "Bring it to me." Frank looked up at the cowboy and snarled under his breath.

The cowboy pulled the money wrapped in a canvass bag, out of the saddlebag and timidly brought it to Johnny Lee. "Honest mister, it weren't my idea to take the money."

"Right, but you still beat the poor man half to death," said Johnny Lee. "And, I'm sure you wouldn't have hesitated helping ol' Frank there spend this money neither. Now, get on back there with the others."

"Ye...yes sir," said the cowboy.

"DOC," Johnny Lee said. "Come out and see to this man's arm."

While he was wrapping Frank Coker's arm the Doctor said, "Not that it bothers me much Frank, you're gonna heal all right. But, the way that bullet tore through your arm, it won't be any use to you as a gun hand anymore." Frank just gritted his teeth in reply.

"Well Frank," said Parker James, "If you're no use to me as a gun hand, I reckon you can collect your severance pay and be movin' on."

"I been loyal to you, doin' yer biddin' for three years and now ya throwin' me out like I was an old dog?"

"Loyal my eye Frank, you ain't loyal to anybody but yourself. Like I said before, I didn't hire you to rob people. I hired you to keep squatters off the open range. So, now just move on, I'll give you a fair severance, but I don't need a man like you on my payroll anymore."

Parker James said to Johnny Lee, "I don't suppose you'd accept a job if I was to offer. I could use a gutsy young fella like you? I'd pay you good."

"I wouldn't even consider working for the likes of you, for no amount of money." said Johnny Lee.

"Well, in that case, I'll give you two days from right now to get yourself and that squatter out of this territory. And, if you don't, I'll have fifty men out here to see to it you move on. I won't be responsible for their unkindness, neither. We don't like squatters or strangers upsetting the balance in these parts."

"Better listen to him, Johnny," said the Doctor. "These ranchers around here can be pretty brutal."

"I'll tell you something, mister," said Johnny Lee. "We'll probably be moving out in the morning. But, if anything was to happen, I'm coming to you. And, I won't be responsible for my unkindness, either. You get my drift?"

"Threaten all you want young man, I could have had you and that squatter shot by now if I had wanted to. Now, be gone with you or face the consequences. And, Doc if I was you, I'd find somewhere else to practice medicine; The Cattlemen's Association won't take kindly to you patchin' up and takin' sides with squatters." Parker James slapped the leads of his horses which jerked the buckboard into motion. "Let's go boys. Two days from now, that's all you got," he said as he and the two cowhands rode away. The Doctor helped Frank Coker on his horse and Frank slowly turned and rode toward town without a word.

"Well, you know Johnny," said the Doctor, "I was getting pretty tired of the prejudice and meanness around here anyway. I'm just not sure which way to go from here though."

"I was thinking about traveling along with Roderick out to California since we were both headed that way anyhow. That is if he doesn't mind. As far as I'm concerned you can join us if you have a mind."

"Sure, I'd like that. I'll slip into town tonight and collect my belongings and close up shop."

The next morning Johnny Lee and the Doctor packed Roderick Travelier's wagon and readied it for the journey to California. Roderick was happy to have Johnny Lee and the Doctor along. After many hours of conversation on the trail Roderick convinced Johnny Lee to invest his money into a vineyard and forget about prospecting since the gold mining business in California had been mostly taken over by big time investors. The two of them formed a very successful partnership and prospered. And, the Doctor sat up practice in the very same area, gave up drinking for the most part, and became a very prominent citizen of the community.

As for Frank Coker, he was shot to death five months later in a saloon fight and Parker James died bankrupt four years later because of bad oil investments.

"Randy. Come little one, wake up. Say good-night to Grandpa and run off to bed. I will come and tuck you in shortly."

"Otay, Grandma. I gonna go pee first."

"It's time for you two to get to bed also. Grandpa's kept you up late enough with his tall tales."

"All right Grandma. But Grandpa, did you know those men you told us about? They did start a vineyard like you and Mr. Thomas, and Doc Hutchinson is a good friend of yours."

"You just never know Tim what good will come if you're a Good Samaritan and help strangers and those in need."

"Wise up Timmy. Won't you ever have a mature mind? Of course, Grandpa knows those men. It's a story about him, Mr. Thomas and Doctor Hutchinson."

"Ah-h, shut up Mary Beth. You don't know, and you're not as smart as you think you are."

"Smarter than any boy like you."

"Enough bickering children, to bed you."

"Alright Grandma. I'm sorry I told you to shut up Mary Beth. Maybe you're right. Good night Grandpa."

"I'm sorry too, Tim. Yes, good night Grandpa."

"Good night children."

"But, is Grandpa's story really about him and the others, Grandma?"

"You know Tim, Grandpa's got a lot of stories and who knows how much of them are true and how much is made up. I think a lot of the time he's just trying to teach you something in his own way. Now don't forget to brush your teeth, I'm going in and help Randy say his prayer. I'll be in to say good night to you two shortly."

THE END

THE LEGEND OF BERT COOK

Bert Cook had become somewhat of a legend to many. As a decorated Infantry Captain in the Confederate Army, military men on both sides had come to respect him. He never asked out of his men something that he would not do himself. He always treated adversaries, including prisoners, fairly and respectfully. Though he didn't necessarily approve of slavery, Bert served the cause the best he could, he was a military man and loved his home in Tennessee. When the war ended however, there was no home to go back to.

The war being over an evil breed of marauding men who did not want to end their careers as killers and plunderers continued on in their violent, rebellious and intimidating ways. They blatantly and brutally robbed, raped and pillaged at will those who would not or could not stand up to them. These were men that had served North and South in the war and for the most part were men of unscrupulous and uncaring nature. To put an end to these ravaging raiders, some state governments and territories appointed Special Agents to track down and deal with this vile element. There was no method or guidelines set as to how the job was to be accomplished, the problem was just to be eliminated so the cry of the citizenry would be calmed. Bert Cook was one of those appointed Special Agents, a Territorial Bounty Hunter.

Bert rode into the desert town of Litchfield Station on a cool, wind-swept and dusty afternoon.

He stopped and tied off his horse in front of the Marshal's Office.

After dismounting and removing his cavalry gloves, Bert slapped the dust out of them on his thigh and tucked them under his belt before entering the door into the little adobe building. He looked around; Bert felt an uneasy quiet, even for a little desert town like this.

Inside, a young man, maybe not even out of his teens, sat at a desk with his head down on folded arms. He jumped and sat up straight when Bert came through the door.

With wide open fearful eyes and a shaky voice he questioned, "Who...who are you?"

"Names Bert Cook. You're not the Marshal here are ya?"

"Me? Heck no. I'm, or...er, was only the deputy."

"Was?"

"Those men, they killed him."

"What men, where? Killed who?"

"Those three settled in down at Crazy Jim's Saloon. Marshal Milton, he was my uncle. They shot him down yesterday, like...like he was nothin'. He's still layin' in the street in front of the saloon where he died. Undertaker's even too scared to go down there."

"Still lyin' there, huh? Now that's plain damned pitiful. Was one of these scum a big man with a red beard, wearin' a Confederate Officer's jacket? Got a foul mouth to go with it?"

"Yeah, that's him all right. Heard he's the one who shot the Marshal."

"Yeah, figures. Butcher," said Bert. "These other two, tell me about them?"

"They're wearin' Johnny Reb outfits too. But, so are you. Yer one of 'em ain't ya?"

"HELL NO boy, I ain't one of 'em. Now, go on, tell me about these fellas."

"Ones, a string bean of a fellow, over six-foot, skinny. And, the other's a small man, smaller 'en me. They're rotten cold killers, all of 'em. Oh-h, I'm sorry mister; they might be friends of yers. You come to join 'em I suppose."

"Quit supposin' and makin' assumptions boy. That kind ain't friends of mine and never will be. Only time I'm friends of vermin like that is when they're lyin' face down in the dirt."

Bert looked around the room and then grabbed a short, double-barreled shotgun that was leaning against the desk and broke it open.

"You're wearin' a Johnny Reb outfit yourself?" questioned the Deputy.

"Just cause we fought on the same side doesn't mean we're the same kind. Like you said, those men are cold-blooded killers for sure. Killed a young fella and carried off his wife whilst robbin' the stage up around Tucson about a week ago. Found the young woman two days ago; pitiable shape she was, dead a'course, prob'ly for the better. Anyway, I tracked them here. What kind of weapons do these men have down there?"

"Heck, I don't know. The little fella's got a rifle of some sort. An...and, they're all totin' big pistols. Other than that, I can't say."

"Where ya keep the shells for this here 10 gauge?"

"In the drawer here," replied the young man. His hand shook uncontrollably as he pulled open the desk drawer and laid a box of buckshot shells on the desk. "I was gonna load it and go down there, but I figgered there was no sense in me gettin' myself killed too. I ain't no match for one man like that, no less three of 'em."

Bert shoved the shotgun into the young man's bosom so that he had to take it and asked, "What's your name son?"

"Ty...Tyrone, Tyrone Myers sir."

"Well, load'r up, Ty...Tyrone. Let me see now, you figured the Marshal was a match for all three of those men by himself...is that it son? Hell boy, they killed your kin, and a lawman at that." Bert paused, as Tyrone fumble with the shells. "Load that damned shotgun boy, and let's get to business down there. That shotgun and the both of us might even the odds a bit."

"The Marshal said, I should stay here," Tyrone whimpered. "And...and he would take care of it by himself. I only done what I was told."

"Yeah all right," said Bert gruffly. "Well, you're wearin' a badge, and I'm tellin' ya to load that shotgun and come on with me."

"Y-es, yes sir." Tyrone reached for the box of shells and knocked them onto the floor. They rolled and scattered about. "Don...don't worry. I'll pick 'em up."

"Hurry up," barked Bert. "We got work ta do."

Tyrone's fingers shook violently as he finally dropped two loads into the barrels. He really did not want any part of this and he wished he would have ripped the tin star off his shirt and thrown it away after the Marshal got shot, but now he couldn't oppose Bert's commanding manner.

"Stuff the rest of those shells in yer pocket. Now, where's this Crazy Jim's place from here?" asked Bert as he motioned Tyrone out the door.

Tyrone stood up, stepped out into the doorway cautiously and pointed down the street with his head. "Just down the street a piece west of here."

"Besides those three no-counts, who else might be in there?"

"Well, they ran Jim out yesterday, right before they killed the Marshal. I think Millie and her son; Millie's Jim's saloon girl, are still down there."

"There's a woman and a kid in there with them?"

"Yeah, but she's just a barmaid, a soiled dove, sort'a speak. She's got a little kid that has no pa or nothin'."

"You ain't much on carin' about people, are ya Tyrone?"

"I don't know sir. I just meant..."

"Yeah. Yeah," interrupted Bert, "I know what you meant. Come on; let's get this takin' care of." Bert stepped out into the street. He wasn't about to let Tyrone out of this, he expected a man to stand on his own two feet, especially when it was to avenge his kin or mete out justice when necessary. He figured Tyrone, was probably pretty proud of that tin star before all of this took place but, now he might be no help at all with little nerve when the showdown came. However, he knew that the presents of two would at least lower the perception of the odds.

With long strides Bert headed down the street. "Come on, Tyrone, keep up," he ordered.

Tyrone followed knowing he had no choice but to do what he was told.

Flies buzzed around the swollen stiff figure lying in the street that had once been an officer of the law. Bert, spat to the side and gritted his teeth in disgust, then he nodded forward. Tyrone stepped up his pace to keep up.

Bert stepped up on the boardwalk in front of the saloon and eased up to the open doorway of Crazy Jim's place and peered inside. The red bearded man that he had referred to as Butcher was standing in front of a table clad in faded flannel underwear with his trousers down around his ankles. The other two men were joking and laughing as they held down a woman on the table. She pleaded in a weak voice as she struggled and kicked to get loose, "No, N-o, not again, not in front of my son".

Oblivious of her pleas Butcher teased, "Hey thar little missy, yer sure 'nough a wild one ain't ya?".

Bert turned briefly to Tyrone and in a low tone said, "Fire that blunder-bust into the ceiling, both barrels." Tyrone just stared, puzzled. "NOW Boy," he whispered through teeth. Tyrone stuck the shot-gun in the door and complied instantly with a thundering blast that brought debris raining down from above. Bert pushed through the swinging doors as he pulled his .44 Remington.

Trying to turn around and reach down for his pistol Butcher, tangle and tripped to the floor getting caught up in his trousers and gun belt.

Two loud smoking explosions, one right after the other, from Bert's .44 sent the two men at the sides of the table to their immediate end. Bert's pistol was now trained on Butcher who was fumbling for his holstered gun on the floor.

"Give it up, Butcher. Yer, done for this day."

"You?" questioned Butcher with a vicious expression. Ignoring the warning he pulled his pistol from its holster.

Bert cocked and pulled the trigger on his Remington. It jammed and miss fired. Now he realized that he should have spent the money for the conversion to a cartridge cylinder.

A wicked grin lit up Butcher's face and his dark eyes blazed with cold spitefulness as he raised his weapon. "We-l-l Cook", he mocked, "Kind'a looks like yer the one that's done for this day. Bye now."

B-O-O-M...a double blast that rattled the walls of the saloon came from the ten gauge shotgun. Butcher jerked and sank into the floor, lifeless. Bert turned to face Tyrone who was holding the smoking double barrel ten gauge. He had reloaded the shotgun after firing into the ceiling. Bert was mighty thankful he had. "We-l-l youngster," he said. "I didn't think you had any grit. Glad I was wrong. Thanks for comin' through." Tyrone looked at Bert for a brief second and smiled slightly then, he dropped the shotgun and ran outside to vomit in the street.

Bert checked his pistol and seen it was fouled with burnt gun power; a bad habit of percussion revolvers of this type, even when they were well maintained by seasoned gunmen like Bert. He holstered it for now and walked over to the table to the sobbing woman. He extended his hand and said, "Come on miss, it's over. No need to fret anymore."

She grabbed his hand and stood up and melted into his arms and held him uncomfortably tight. In a breathless low voice she said, "Thank you mister, I sure didn't want my son to witness what that horrible man was about to do again." She buried her face into Bert's chest and tried to get her breath back as she silently wept.

Then Bert felt a tightening around his leg just above his knee and when he looked down he saw a full head of blond hair. A shy round young face with big light brown eyes looked up into his. "Thank you, sir for saving my mommy from that mean, mean man." The boy had come from the end of the bar where he had been crouching down in fear watching his mother's abuse.

Bert reached down and stroked the back of the boys head. "Yer surely welcome youngin."

The young woman released her grip on Bert and took a half step back. She sniffed, composed herself, leaned down and caressed her sons face tenderly. "This is my son, Raymond," she said.

Bert bent down on one knee to make himself eye level with Raymond and extended a hand to shake. Raymond took his hand and he said, "I'm Bert Cook. Good ta meet you, Raymond."

Raymond looked up at his mom and said, "Mommy, I like Bert Cook, I like him a lot."

She bent down beside Bert and opened her arms to her son. He responded and she hugged him tightly. "I love you so much Raymond," she wept softly.

"I love you too, Mommy. No need to cry, Bert Cook took care of those mean men."

She looked up at Bert, who was now standing again. "He sure did, son," she said. "Thank you ever so much Mister Cook."

"No need for thanks. The Deputy and me just did what needed to be done."

Tyrone who had recovered from his episode outside and came up to them and said, "I guess we did take care of business, huh Mister Cook?"

"Well, Tyrone I reckon we did. And you sure enough earned the right to hang that star on yer shirt." Tyrone smiled in response. "Don't get too cocky son. Over confidence can kill ya just sure as anything," said Bert.

"Is there a telegraph office here about?" asked Bert.

"Shore," said Tyrone, "Down the street in the train station, right across from Johnson's Livery Stables."

"Well then, how 'bout you get somebody to take care of these bodies while I'll take care of some business down at the train station," said Bert.

"Shore 'nough Mister Cook," said Tyrone.

"Call me Bert, Deputy."

"All right, Bert, I'll get it done," assured Tyrone.

Bert turned to leave; the young woman reached and touched his arm for his attention. He turned and caught her deep brown sparkling eyes penetrating his very being. A captivating, yet uneasy feeling came over him, something that he did not recognize or had ever experienced before, it settled in the pit of his stomach. The feeling seemed to control him; something that Bert never let anything do.

"I'm Millie Kinsley, Mister Cook. Will I see you again?"

Bert's plan was to telegraph Tucson for the three-hundred dollar reward money, wait for it to arrive and move on to the next quest, however now he felt himself uncomfortably compelled to linger.

"Well, ma'am I was plannin' to move on in a couple days after I had collected the reward money for those three varmints."

"I bet you haven't had a real home cooked meal in a while. I'd like to have you join Raymond and me at the supper table this evening. Jim, the owner of this saloon, provides me with a little cottage out back. Seven o'clock, Apple Pie. What do you say? I mean it's the least I can do for what you did today. Please do come."

"You sure make it hard to say no, mame."

"Then say yes and please call me, Millie," she said.

"Well," said Bert, "if you will call me Bert, I'd be happy to supper with you and Raymond."

"Wonderful Bert, seven o'clock then."

Later at supper Bert found Millie easy to talk to. Millie told him about coming to Litchfield Station, with a young gambler she had run off with from Carson City, her home town, he was Raymond's father. Shortly after they arrived in town she found she was pregnant and not long after that the young gambler was caught cheating at a stud poker game. He drew a knife on his angry accuser who pulled a pocket pistol and shot him twice in the stomach. He suffered three days before dying of his wounds. The Circuit Judge later ruled it self-defense and the man left town shortly after the inquiry. She was left alone with nothing, so Jim gave her a job and a place for her and the baby to stay. That had been eight years earlier and she pretty well ran Crazy Jim's now that he involved himself in local politics and the Town Council.

Bert seldom ever talked about himself or his past but, he found he was telling Millie about the home he had in Tennessee. How after the war there was nothing left, and how he had come to be in this town on this particular day. They talked into the night, even after little Raymond, who had become very attached to Bert, had gone to bed. Bert who was forty-four years old found out that Millie was twenty-five.

When Bert was finally ready to leave for the night, Millie embraced him tenderly by sliding her arms around his neck. Bert responded and found great comfort and serenity in having this young woman in his arms. Their faces close as their eyes drew them together, Bert's strong breathing took the young woman's breath and they slipped into a passionate kiss. Bert had never felt this way about a woman before; though his mind was fighting it, his heart was giving in to the strong feelings he was having for Millie.

"I would like to see you again, Bert?" she whispered, her tender lips skimming his as she spoke softly. "It's been a most pleasant evening; thank you ever so much for coming," she said.

They separated slightly. "Well, I'm sure we'll see one another again," Bert said. "I had a good evening as well. Thanks for the great meal."

"Wonderful, I look forward to it. Raymond likes you so well. You are really good for him."

"He's a good kid, and I like him too. Well, bye for now," Bert said.

"Yes, bye Bert," Millie said.

Bert stayed at the local hotel that night and early the next day while he was eating breakfast at Jenny's White Front Restaurant next door, Crazy Jim, a huge man over six foot, and three other members of the Town Council sat down to talk. After brief introductions, they very strongly urged him to take on the vacant Town's Marshal's job. They assured him he was the man for the job of keeping order in their town. They also strongly emphasized that the pay was twenty dollars a month, plus room and board at the hotel and, fifty cents for every arrest with a conviction.

Before meeting Millie, Bert would have never considered settling in to a town job, he preferred the wide open spaces but, now it seemed a tempting offer. Maybe it was time to settle down a bit, he wasn't getting any younger and the trails and men he had to deal with were getting harder. Bert hesitated giving an answer right away stating he would give it some thought. In response, The Town Council's spokesman quickly and insistently, offered twenty-two dollars a month.

Bert pretty well doubted they would go for it, so he countered, "Make it, twenty-five a month and sixty cents an arrest conviction and you've got a deal."

The Council member's looked at each other and after a brief pause said, "Alright, if you will sign a two year contract, we'll do it." All agreed and over the big smiles and head shaking of the Town Council members they all shook hands. Two days later Bert made Tyrone take a hundred dollars of the reward money for the three men they had killed a few days prior. He also asked Tyrone to remain on as his Deputy; Tyrone accepted and went on to become a pretty reliable lawman himself.

Six months after taking on the job of Town Marshal, Bert began to feel quite comfortable in his new life style. He enjoyed the respect many in town gave him and thought his life was set.

The job was not the only thing Bert had gotten comfortable with. Bert and Millie visited and talked almost every day, so they got married; it just seemed like the right thing to do at the time. Not everyone felt the same though, many of the towns folk raised eyebrows of skepticism, mostly due to their age difference, and Millie's reputation as a woman of immoral nature. Bert spent a lot of time taking Raymond fishing, hunting and teaching the young lad how to track and live in the wilderness. Raymond and Bert were bonding and soon became almost inseparable.

Bert held tight reins on the town and stepped on not just a few of the prominent rancher's toes by arrest and fines of their cowhands. Most arrest was disorderly conduct for fighting or public drunkenness; there were a few arrests for public lewdness for urinating in the street. About eighteen months after Bert became Marshal the Town Council, decided it was time to appoint a Mayor over the town. They decided on Council Member, Theodore J. Moser, the wealthiest cattleman in the valley, as the first Mayor of Litchfield Station.

Moser and his family were also the biggest critics of Marshal Cook's tactics and there was no love lost between them and Bert, seeing how a large percentage of the cowboys he arrested were from their spread. Not to mention the fact that Mrs. Moser was the head founder of the Women's Social Club and Millie was the most often subject of her gossip in the ladies sewing circle.

Moser's youngest of five boys was Jake and he and Bert had locked horns more than once. Jake's father always came and bailed him out. Jake was also quite a ladies' man and had caught the interest of Millie on a number of occasions even though he was a few years younger than her.

When not out with Raymond, Bert spent most of his time in Crazy Jim's playing poker and sipping rye whiskey. He had noticed the attraction between the two, however, up until now he had written it off as part of Millie's job as a saloon girl.

Besides, Bert wasn't the jealous type nor easily riled. That however came to an abrupt end one early afternoon after Bert came in from fishing with Raymond and found Millie was not home. Millie had figured Bert and Raymond would not be back until almost dark so she was spending time playfully flirting with Jake in the saloon.

When Bert entered Crazy Jim's from the rear door and saw the two of them kidding around and laughing, his bristles came up. Then when Millie seductively kissed Jake and passionately embraced him wrapping one leg around him, Bert could only see red. "ENOUGH," called Bert. They both turned toward him and froze in place. Bert walked up to the couple and said, "Get your damned hands off my wife you stupid kid." The fifteen or so patrons in the saloon now had all their attention on the three of them.

"We were just funning around, Bert," said Millie.

Bert grabbed Millie's arm and jerked her away from Jake. "Sure you were; I saw what you were doing. Now, get your butt home and take care of yer son."

"You don't own me, Bert Cook," said Millie. Bert still had a hold on her arm and he powerfully shoved her toward the back door. She tried to resist which only caused her to stumbled and fall to the floor really hard. Jake started to step in and was met with a potent backhand from Bert that sent him bouncing against the bar and then to join Millie on the floor. Bert grabbed Millie's arm again and lifted her up to her feet, then he turned and pointed a fisted finger at Jake and said, "You ever touch my wife again and I'll shoot you down like a cur dog. Boy, you do understand." Bert wasn't asking Jake a question, he was making a statement. In return all he got was a cold stare from the young man after he spit blood on the floor and pushed himself upright. With that Bert forcefully marched Millie home, she struggled unsuccessfully while cursing and kicking all the way.

Not much was heard from Bert, but you could hear Millie's screaming and things breaking for about a half hour before Bert finally left for the Marshal's Office. There Bert kicked Tyrone out for the evening and grabbed an almost full bottle of rye whiskey out of the desk drawer. He uncorked it and poured three fingers in a glass which he downed in one gulp, and then he followed it with several more. Bert and the bottle spent the night together.

After a few weeks things seemed to calm down and get back to a relative normal state, Millie and Bert had tentatively made up and things seemed to be on the mend. Then one evening about two month after the last incident Bert had been drinking all afternoon and was playing poker with four other locals when he heard Millie laughing and giggling a few tables away. He hadn't realized that Jake had come into Crazy Jim's twenty minutes or so earlier, if he had he would have kept an eye on him or just kicked him out.

Bert could not see where Millie was from where he was sitting, so he just kind of ignored the giggling at first, after all she was supposed to entertain and encourage the cowboys to drink up.

The laughing and commotion kept getting louder and more excited, Bert needed to know what was going on. He raised himself up from his chair and looked over the shoulder of the player sitting across from him. What Bert saw sent him into a blind rage, he kicked his chair out from behind him sending it flying against the wall and breaking it into pieces. He started for Millie and Jake with white hot blazing eyes. Millie was sitting on Jake's lap laughing and teasing with him, his hand was up her dress between her thighs. When the two saw Bert coming their laughter stopped abruptly and Millie stood up. When Bert was about two steps away she shouted, "NO." He shoved her aside and stood over Jake setting in the chair.

With narrowed, cold and mean eyes he said, "You don't learn, do ya sonny? I told you what would happen the next time you touched my wife."

Jake leaned back in his chair, a big grin filled his face; drunk, he was oblivious of the seriousness of the situation. Jake snickered and said, "What, Bert? We was jess funnin', no need ta be so cross."

Millie yelled again, "NO BERT...DON'T."

Bert pulled his .44 and aimed at the young man's chest point blank. No misfire this time, Bert had changed his Remington to a cartridge conversion. BOOM— Jake spilled over backwards in his chair, lifeless. Millie, tears streaming down her face started pounding on Bert's shoulder with her fist screaming, "How could you...how could you do this?"

Then Tyrone, who was on door check duty, pushed through the saloon doors with the 10 gauged leveled. After a few steps insides he stopped, he saw that everyone was looking Bert's way. "What in hell happened here?" he said.

A trio of answers came all saying the same thing, 'Bert shot and killed Jake in cold blood.'

Tyrone looked at Bert with bewildered eyes, "Bert?"

Millie melted to the floor sobbing uncontrollably. Bert looked down at her and said, "Tell Raymond, I'm sorry we won't be goin' fishin' no more. And...and tell him I love him. I love you too, Millie." With that Bert jammed the Remington back in place, turned and headed for the door.

As Bert approached, Tyrone said, "Bert, do I arrest you?"

"Stand down for now, Deputy. If anyone wants me, I'll be in the cabin at Rawlins Mill stream. There's a full moon tonight; if I see anybody before mornin' they'll end up like Jake." Bert paused briefly, his expression softened and he looked deep into Tyrone's eyes. Bert had become a mentor and like a father to Tyrone. "You know I mean what I say; don't ya Deputy?" said Bert.

"Yes I do, Bert."

"Yer a good man, Tyrone. Tomorrow you do your duty as an officer of the law. Be seein' ya, Deputy." Bert yanked the tin star off his vest and tossed it on a nearby a table, then he walked out of the saloon into the night.

A group of cowboys started clamoring about getting a rope. Tyrone knew he had to squelch this quick or he was going to have an uncontrollable lynch party on his hands. He said, "Listen here ya all, you heard what Bert said."

"Yeah, well Deputy," said one cowboy, "He'll be long gone by mornin', so we need to get after him tonight." The crowd murmured in agreement.

"Ya all might think a lot of things about Bert Cook but, one thing I know for sure, he's a man of his word. He'll be where he says he'll be in the mornin'. Ain't no sense anybody goin' out there tonight and getting' all shot up. Beside, ain't no one gonna do any lynchin' in this town. I'll arrest any damned fool who tries. This will all be done according to the law. We can all use the night to get our thinkin' straight and deal with this in the mornin'."

A cowboy spoke up and said, "Yeah the Deputy's right, besides, Jake's brothers are gonna want to be in on this."

"All right then," said Tyrone, "let's break this up for tonight and meet here in the mornin' around six. We'll go out and get this deal taken care of. Ya all go and get some rest, tomorrow is gonna be a long day. The crowd agreed for the most part and they started talking among themselves and leaving Crazy Jim's.

Bert arrived at the cabin around midnight. As he dismounted he pulled his rifle out of the scabbard and grabbed the saddlebags and took them inside. He went back out and stripped his horse of the saddle and all the rest of the gear and turned the horse loose knowing it would wonder back into town. Then he took everything inside the cabin.

Bert pulled his extra pistol out of his saddle bag, it was a new Smith & Wesson Model No.3 he had ordered a few months back, he had thought about retiring his Remington but just could not do it. He checked the action and then loaded it with fresh cartridges and then he did the same with the Remington .44 on his hip. He grabbed the rifle, checked and loaded it also, then set it next to the window. Bert started a fire in the little stove in the cabin and put together a pot of coffee. He found a tin cup and blew the dust out of it before pouring it half full of rye whiskey. After the coffee was hot he added some more rye to the cup and topped it off with coffee. Then he sliced some bacon he had brought and filled a skillet with a half dozen pieces.

Bert chewed on the bacon after it was ready and sipped on the coffee, whiskey mix. He sat silently in thought until it started getting day light.

About an hour after day break a posse of twelve to fifteen men lead by Deputy Tyrone Myers came from town riding the road that ran along a mountain stream down beside the old Rawlins' Mill. Just beyond the mill, about a quarter of a mile or so, sat an abandon cabin that anyone could use when they were up that way hunting, fishing or whatever the need was. When they came within about a hundred yards of the cabin a window pane broke out from within the cabin and a rifle shot buzzed over the groups head. Everyone but Tyrone scurried off the road to seek cover, dismount and draw their weapons. The cowboys and the Moser brothers started firing at the cabin from behind the rocks and trees where they had ducked for cover.

Sitting erect in the saddle Tyrone commanded, "Hold yer fired." All complied and looked to him for further instructions. This wasn't the same young man that Bert had pushed into action back when he first arrived in town. He had matured and learned to take on responsibilities under Bert's tutoring.

Tyrone dismounted, pulled a Colt from his belt and checked the load. Then he put it back in his belt. "BERT," he called, "Hold up, I'm coming in." He turned his head toward the men hiding in the bushes, "Ya all hold yer fire and wait here til I get back." Tyrone started for the cabin.

Most expected Bert would shoot Tyrone when he got close to the cabin, but they just did not understand Bert Cook the way he did.

Tyrone stopped and stood at the door. "Well, come ahead," said Bert, "You've got this far." Tyrone stepped inside. Bert was sitting in a chair watching out the window.

"Not a good day for me Bert," Tyrone said.
"Well, sorry about that Deputy," said Bert. "You just do yer job and it'll come out right."

"You know what I have to do," said Tyrone.

"Shore, I know. Don't hold it agin ya at all," Bert said.

"Well...Do we smoke ya out? Or, will ya come along peaceful. I'll see to it you'll get a fair trial," said Tyrone.

"I know ya will," said Bert. "But, we both know how that'll come out. And, I been thinkin' on that most of the mornin'. Here's what I'm gonna do my young friend, you go on back out there with those fine town folks and I'll be coming out shortly.

I just got one more little bit of thinkin' alone I need ta do before I come."

"All right," said Tyrone. "Yer comin' out…But yer not gonna do nothin' stupid are ya?"

"Tyrone, I'm a man who has always done what has to be done and I ain't about to change," said Bert.

Tyrone said, "Alright Bert. Ten minutes gonna do?"

"Ten minutes will be fine. Ten minutes and I'll be headin' yer way," said Bert.

"Okay Bert," said Tyrone as he turned and opened the door. "And Bert, be best if ya leave yer shootin' ir'ns in here." Tyrone started the walk back to where everyone was waiting.

"What's it gonna be, Deputy?" said one of Jake's brothers.

"He asked for ten minutes and we're gonna give him that," said Tyrone. "He'll be out shortly." Tyrone pulled out his pocket watch and noted the time.

Almost to the second by Tyrone's watch, Bert yelled and swung open the door. "Al'm a comin' out boys, and I intend to take some of ya with me." With that Bert ran from the doorway full force toward their location with both pistols blazing. Nobody but Tyrone, who stood in the wide open, realized Bert was shooting off to the side and over their heads. Every man's gun but Tyrone's spoke loud until Bert lay in the dirt motionless.

—

"Well, Mr. Pedicort that's the real story."

"That is not quite the way everyone else around here tells the story of Bert Cook, Sheriff. What I have heard numerous times is that he was a bully, an abusive wife beater and a cold blooded killer," said Pedicort.

"You can think and write what you want, I mean, it is your magazine. What I'm telling you is the truth and what really happened in old Litchfield Station and with Bert Cook."

Pedicort said, "What makes you such an expert? Am I supposed to believe you just because you're County Sheriff? Why should I believe you over most of the people who live in the valley?"

"Well, M-ister Pedicort, for one thing I was Sheriff Ty Myers Deputy, for over thirteen years. Second, I might just actually know the real story because Millie Kinsley-Cook was my mother."

"But your last name is Chaney, not Kinsley," said Pedicort.

"That's right, my name is Ray Chaney. I was named by my mother at birth after my father, Raymond Phillip Chaney," said Sheriff Chaney.

"Well, that makes all the difference in the world. I suppose you can prove Millie was your mother?" said Pedicort.

"Sure I can, but I'm not going to," said Sheriff Chaney. "That's your job if you want to write about Bert Cook and tell the real story. The way I see it, it's not just Bert's reputation that is at stake here, so is the reputation of your magazine. So, asked yourself Mr. Pedicort, do you want to go down to the Court House and do the research or do you want to go on people's assumptions and predigest?"

"You know Sheriff Chaney," said Pedicort, "you're right. I want the historic truth. I am going to do the research. Thanks." Pedicort reached across the desk and shook Sheriff Chaney's hand and then left the office.

Six months later in 'The Historic West' magazine:

"The Legend of Bert Cook"
as related to me by Sheriff Raymond Chaney
—Stanford J. Pedicort—

JERRY'S NEW COWBOY HAT

It had been a long hard last week of work and Jerry was glad to finally get into town on Saturday morning. He had wrestled with that old windmill for four days, doing most of the work by himself, but he finally got it going. He must have climbed up and down that rigging five hundred times; at least that's what it felt like, and then he had broken three saddle horses on Friday. These were things Jerry promised Mr. Vega would get done before he severed his employment with him, and he was a man of his word to the letter.

Jerry and Debbie had been saving for seven years and now they had enough money to buy the old Stevens' place. They had deprived themselves of many things and worked hard; Jerry as Vega's number one hand and Debbie as the Vega's cook and part time housekeeper. This, Debbie did after a full day of teaching at the grade school. It was all worth it now; they had saved enough to have a ranch home they could call their own. All that remained was for Jerry to draw the money out of the bank and sign the final papers and it would be all settled.

The bank didn't open until ten o'clock on Saturday, so Jerry bought some supplies for his new home over at the General Store. However, he still had another forty-five minutes to wait before the bank would open so he could finalize his business. He decided he would go over to the Flat Iron Saloon until ten and have some coffee and talk cows and breeding with some of the other ranchers he knew would be there on a Saturday morning.

Jerry was of slight stature, yet solid for five foot six. He was easy going in nature and had worked hard all his life and was respected by most everyone in town as one who could take a stand if pushed hard enough. Jerry had afforded himself and Debbie one luxury each at the General Store that morning; Debbie a new blue, chiffon trimmed, dress and himself a much needed new Texas cowboy hat.

As Jerry headed toward the Flat Iron from the General Store he proudly custom shaped his new hat, trying it on and then reshaping it again to fit his taste. As he stepped up on the boardwalk, to enter the Flat Iron Saloon, he felt he had it just right. This hat would last him a long time and serve him well, protecting him from the scorching Arizona sun as well as the rain and other elements of the desert Southwest. Jerry, like most cowboys, formed an attachment to a new hat quickly. It was more than just a tool of the trade. A hat would reflect a man's personality by the way he shaped it and wore it just so on his head. He had formed a kinship with this particular hat already; it had just spoken to him sitting there on the shelf at the General Store. It was hard replacing his old hat, but it was time. Debbie had nagged him about the old hat long enough. "It just doesn't look good on Sunday with your suit," (the only suit he had), she would say. The old hat had been stepped on by cows, dropped in manure piles more times than anyone would care to count, and then it had been kicked by various horses, whilst Jerry's head was still in it of course, but it still maintained its character.

Bruce Douglass, the owner of the General Store, had insistently offered to dispose of his old hat for him. "We-ll," said Jerry, "I'll just keep the old one around a little while longer, to do chores and such." So Jerry had tossed his old companion in the back of the buckboard before heading for the Flat Iron.

After he entered the saloon, he paused a few moments to let his eyes adjust to the dimmer light. He looked around to see who was there. Three locals, two cowboys and Elijah Gibson the chairman of the Cattlemen's Association, sat playing poker with a broad shouldered, woolly looking stranger. Frank Courson, whom Jerry knew quite well, stood at the bar drinking a beer.

Frank had a fair sized spread just a mile or so west of town. He had done a lot of prize-winning breeding and Jerry liked talking with him so he could learn all that he could about the subject. As soon as Frank and the others looked up to see who it was, they all took note of the new hat and poked a little lighthearted fun at him, which he took in stride.

The big stranger looked at Jerry with narrowed mean eyes and spoke out harshly about the interruption of the poker game. "You, yeah-hoo's gonna play poker or cackle over that ugly hat like a bunch of old women?" Jerry gently lifted the hat off his head and looked it over, shrugged and place it carefully back on his head. Jerry didn't like the strangers comment about his new hat, but he didn't feel it was worth causing a stir and maybe ruining the day by making an issue over it. So, he just walked over to the bar to join Frank and ordered a cup of coffee.

Frank and Jerry were just getting immersed in a conversation about choosing a good bull for breeding, when the big stranger stood up boisterously proclaiming his victory in the poker game. He stood well over six-foot tall with broad shoulders and an irritating loud intimidating bellowing gravel voice. "I shore hope you boy's drink better'n ya play poker," the big man said. "If ya ain't the worst bunch of poker players I've ev'r seen, then yer shore 'nough next to it. To show my appreciation fer yer sorry playin'.... Barkeep," he said, "Whiskey all around, fer ev'rbody in the place. I skinned these yeahoo's pretty darn good." With that the big stranger walked over to the bar and stood beside Jerry.

The barkeeper took a bottle and three glasses over to the poker table and poured each man there a drink. After he returned to his place behind the bar he set two glasses up, one in front of Frank and one in front of Jerry. He poured Frank's and then started to pour Jerry's. Jerry put his hand over the glass and shook his head. "Not today…Coffee's good enough for me, Vern."

"O-h…All right, Jerry," said Vern the barkeep.

"No…No. Go ahead little fella, al'm a buyin," said the big man as he heartily slapped Jerry across the back. "And, when Cain Mormon sets up whiskey, ev'rbody drinks. S-o, go ahead, throw one down ner."

Jerry turned to face Cain and when he did he was looking into the big man's chest. Jerry looked up into the man's hard, unyielding eyes. He said, "Well mister, it's like this. Whiskey doesn't set well with me, and I got some business to take care of in a bit. So, I wanna keep a clear head. Thanks just the same, but coffee suites me better today." Jerry turned back and started his conversation with Frank again.

The big man wasn't going to let this rest. Cain's eyes burned dark with hostility. Forcefully loud he said, "I guess ya don't hear too good, runt. I said, when Cain Mormon buys ev'rbody drinks." Jerry's hair was up on his neck now, but he ignored the man's bullying.

"I'd be careful who you are callin' names there, stranger," said Vern from behind the bar. "Jerry don't take kindly to that kind of talk you know?"

"What's yer name, runt? Jerry WHO?" said Cain.

Jerry turned slowly and answered, "Jerry Grace is my name. And look, I'd let this go now if I were you." Jerry turned his back on the big man for the second time.

Cain's expression was an inferno of rage now and he slapped Jerry in the back of the head, knocking Jerry's new hat off his head. On its way to the floor Jerry's hat hit a cuspidor knocking it over.

"Yer no man if ya can't stomach whiskey, runt. So barkeep, fill that 'ere glass plum full."

"I won't do that mister," said Vern. The big man backhanded Vern across the mouth.

That was it for Jerry, he had enough of the big man's bullying, he turned around and started poking his finger sharply into the big man's chest. "Who do you think you are comin' in here pushin' folks around. If you don't settle down I'm gon..." Jerry froze, his eyes glazed white hot at the sight of his brand new cowboy hat lying in a puddle of thick, brown, slimy goo beside the cuspidor.

As Jerry had looked away, Cain's hand went down to a .45 Colt Army he had holstered at his side. Jerry had given up carrying a six-gun, except out on the range a number of years before, so he was unarmed. However, before Cain could bring his pistol up, Vern had both barrels of a sawed off shotgun cocked and pointed at his head. "There will be no gun play in here big fella."

Jerry turned to face Cain as the big man carefully laid his pistol on the bar. "I don't need a shootin' ir'n to deal with this runt anyways," said Cain. With that Cain reached out and grabbed two fists full of the front of Jerry's shirt and hefted him up off of his feet. Jerry's feet dangled in the air as Cain threatened, "Al'm gonna crush you like the little chigger you are, little man."

Jerry cupped his hands and boxed Cain's ears as hard as he could. As he did he felt the front of his shirt give and rip on both sides. Cain grunted and dropped Jerry to the floor. Cain shook his head violently and was regaining his senses when Jerry reared back his right foot and kicked ol' Cain hard, right square in his shin. Then, before the big man had time to react to that, Jerry kicked again, even harder than the first time. Cain grabbed his leg with both hands and toppled to the floor in a heap of moaning jelly.

"O-o-h...I think ya broke my dad-burn leg," whined Cain.

Jerry took a firm hold of Cain's right ear between his fingers and said, "Now, listen here, Mis-ter Mormon. You are going to pick up my hat out of that slop, and you and me are going to march over to the General Store, where you are going to pay Mr. Douglass over there to clean my hat.

"Then you're gonna come back here, get your gun and ride out of town, and never show your face around here again." Jerry gave Cain's ear a hardy twist. "Now, is that agreeable to you, Mi-s-ter Mormon?"

Cain cringed his face tightly and answered, "Yea...Yes sir. That's agreeable."

"Good. Stand up here, and let's go." After Cain picked up the hat he tried to stand erect but, could not because of Jerry's shorter height. Jerry led him toward the door of the saloon all bent over and limping severely. As they passed by the other men in the bar chuckled and said, "Ya just don't mess with Jerry's new cowboy hat."

Still holding tightly to Cain's ear Jerry lead him across the street to the General Store.

When Jerry came home that evening, he held the box with the new blue, chiffon trimmed dress in front of him so Debbie wouldn't notice his torn shirt. After their greeting, Jerry held the box out to her. "This is for you my dear. You've wanted this for quite a spell now, and I thought you deserved it since we had a little extra."

"O-h-h, Jerry. For me?" she said. She excitedly went right to opening it. "O-h-h, I love it. It's so pretty. Thank you dear," she said. She went to give him a hug, and that's when she noticed the torn shirt. "JERRY. What happened to your shirt? Have you been fighting? You know how I feel about you fighting. You've been in the Flat Iron, haven't you? Oh, I ha-t-e that place. Is that why you bought me this dress?"

"N-o-w, now, calm down dear. I can explain everything, if you just give me a minute."

Debbie cocked her head slightly and raised an eyebrow, "You have a new hat?" she said.

"Yes. Yes I do. You have been wanting me to get a new hat, so I did. Yes, I bought me a brand spankin' new cowboy hat. Don't you like it?" said Jerry pleasantly. He was sure glad the conversation had been sidetracked from the ruckus at the Flat Iron.

"But how did a brand new hat get that light brown stain around the brim already?" she said.

Bruce Douglass at the General Store had done all that he could to clean the new hat but he just could not remove all of that stain. It was ever so light, but it still showed. Jerry felt, it kind of gave it character. Especially since he had taken down a man the size of Cain to get it that way.

Jerry sat Debbie down and explained his whole day to her and though she was a little irritated she got over it quickly. Mostly, because Jerry had finalized the papers at the bank and she was very pleased with her new home and of course her new blue, chiffon trimmed, dress. The couple fixed the old Stevens' place up real nice and settled in it quickly. Cain Mormon was never heard of around there again. Jerry wore that hat for many a year and found it just as hard to replace as he had his old one previously. Now, the Grace family have become respected and successful ranchers in the area and their family has grown to include two lovely daughters, Sarah and Adele, and they all live very happy lives together.

THE END

Dedicated to my Dear friend Jerry Grace and Family

BEHIND THE BADGE

Sheriff Roman Austin sat sipping black coffee, anticipating his Monday morning breakfast. Suddenly, the front door to Kate Sellers' Restaurant slammed open with a hard bang. The glass strained almost to the point of breaking. Doc Flagg stood in the doorway searching through squinted, bloodshot eyes. He focused on Roman Austin the Sheriff in town. He opened his eyes wide and squinted again as he stumbled toward the table. The Doctor literally fell down in a chair across from the Sheriff and rested his arm on the table. He sighed and relaxed, nearly falling out of the chair. Then he tightened his bushy white eyebrows and shook his head as if seriously confused.

"What's going on there, Doc?" said the Sheriff. "You look a bit rattled."

Doc Flagg held up his palm and shook his head. "N…no, Rom'," he said struggling for breath. "In a minute, okay?"

"We-ll? To what do we owe this honor, Doc?" Kate Sellers said, who had come over to the table. "You never come in here before noon."

Bending down Kate noticed the look on Doc Flagg's face. "What on earth's wrong with you, Doc? You're as white as a ghost, whiter than usual anyway."

"Give me [cough] coffee," said Doc Flagg. "Give me a cup of black coffee. Ge…[cough] give me two cups of black coffee."

"Sure Doc," said Kate and she hurried off.

"Somebody shut that front door," said Kate as she headed for the kitchen to get the coffeepot.

Doc Flagg reached into his wrinkled tweed coat pocket and pulled out a stub of a cigar. Then he struck a match on his shoe and lit it, almost burning his nose. Doc's face disappeared in a puff of smoke. As the smoke cleared he coughed and cleared phlegm in his throat. "I never thought I'd see the day," he said looking bewildered.

"What Doc?" Roman said insistently. "What's your problem this morning?"

Before Doc could answer, Kate was back with the large coffeepot and a cup. She sat the cup in front of Doc and poured; she filled Roman's cup also. Then she sat the big pot on the floor and seated herself beside Roman. Thoughtfully, Kate reached over and squeezed Doc Flagg's hand gently. He put his hand on top of hers and smiled appreciatively.

"What's got you shook so, Doc?" Kate said softly.

"We-ll," said Doc, "I'll tell ya. You'd be shook up too, if you'd seen what I saw this mawnin'."

"All right Doc," Roman said impatiently, "Enough mystery. What did you see?"

"I'll tell ya," said Doc Flagg sharply, "I'll tell ya what I saw. I went over to the Lucky Lady this mawnin', to get a hair-of-the-dog, an' there, at the foot of the stairs, laid ol' Horace Pape in a river of blood. I m-ean…Shoo," Doc just shook his head.

Doc Flagg coughed and gasped as he struck another match to the little stub of a cigar again. Kate grabbed the stub out of his mouth leaving him scowling and holding the match.

"DOC," said Kate. "You're gonna sit yourself on fire there. Besides, those things are killin' you anyway." Doc Flagg squinted, giving her a curious nod.

Sheriff Austin's patience was wearing thin. "Well- Is he dead?" said the Sheriff.

Turning back to Roman, Doc said, "Damned right he's dead, Rom'. I am a doctor ya know."

Controlling his impatience Roman said, "All right, Doc. Did you touch anything or move anything?"

"Heck no, Rom'," said Doc. "Don't ya think I know better'n that. Now, ought'n you go down there and conduct an inquiry or somethin'; instead of settin' around here askin' fool questions? Heck man, he was your friend too."

"Yeah Doc, I should. Let's go."

Sheriff Austin took a last sip of hot coffee. Doc Flagg mirrored the Sheriff's actions and with a determined look, the two of them headed toward the door.

"I reckon I'll save fixing your breakfast 'til later," said Kate as Roman snatched his hat off the rack and hurried through the door.

"Good idea, Kate," he said.

Doc Flagg practically ran to keep up with Roman as he strutted with jaw set and eyes straight ahead. Roman kept this sober expression the whole two blocks to the Lucky Lady Saloon.

Other than a few shopkeepers, busying themselves with sweeping the walks and setting up displays of their wares, Main Street Bristle Bush was deserted. All the shopkeepers greeted the hurried pair with, "Good morning Sheriff...Doc." They received little or no response from the two, which earned them a curious, unappreciative stare.

Horace Pape had changed the name of Pape's Palace Saloon, to The Lucky Lady Saloon, after marrying a pretty, twenty-six year old dance hall girl named, Roxanne. Horace hired Roxanne and fell deeply in love with her shortly thereafter. Horace felt having her around had changed his luck for the better. However, Roxanne was a gold-digger and had won the hearts of more than just Horace. Love and beauty blinded this fifty five year old saloon keeper to the fact that the love of his life had no moral scruples whatsoever, or maybe he just didn't care as long as she belonged to him. Whichever the case, there was little or no fidelity on her part.

Horace Pape had been the reason Roman Austin came to Bristle Bush, Arizona in the first place. Horace and Roman had served in the Army together, fighting Indians for a number of years before Horace, left the military and bought the saloon.

Sheriff Austin played a major role in the peacefulness and order that abided in and around the town. The town was only about a third of what it had been when Roman had arrived almost eleven years earlier. Now, all the mines had closed down, except for the Peterson & Doggett Silver and Gold Mining Company.

After the Indian wars, Roman left the Army and came to Bristle Bush to settle down and make a home for himself. However, this wild and woolly mining community was in need of law and order, and Roman Austin had been the only one with the experience and willingness to take on the job. So when asked, he accepted and started right in on the task at hand. In short order he earned the respect of the people he had to deal with on a daily basis.

The miners, who were a rough and tumble breed, only understood and respected someone who could deal with them on their own level, and Roman was certainly the man that could stand up to the challenge. Sheriff Austin bent a pistol barrel over a few rowdy miner's head and had taken more than one, who thought he was tough down, a notch or two. It wasn't long before things settled down and the town had the respectability it needed to make real progress. Nowadays however, with the mines gone except one, there were only a handful of miners left, and they were seldom any trouble.

Being an ex-military officer, Roman felt a lawman should have a professional appearance, so he always dressed well. A suit, with a long coat, a white collared shirt with a black string tie and high top, spit shined black boots. All this was accented by two bone handled nickel plated Colts that hung heavy at his sides; all of this was his usual attire.

Roman was still in the lead when he and Doc entered the Lucky Lady Saloon. Roman moved cautiously down the length of the brass trimmed mahogany bar; Doc Flagg held back a bit. Across from the back end where the bar opened, was a stairway that led up to four rooms. At the foot of the stairs lay the lifeless body of the saloonkeeper, Horace Pape. Roman bent down and slowly rolled the lifeless body of his friend over.

"How long you reckon he's been dead, Doc?" Roman asked.

"From the condition of the body now, I'd suppose, no more than three or four hours."

"Looks like a large knife wound to me, Doc?"

"I'd say that's a pretty fair conclusion," Doc Flagg said as he looked over the fatal wound. "Severed a major artery looks like. He died quick."

Roman looked up the stairs and said, "Where…where is Roxanne?"

"Don't know. Ain't seen her around, Rom'. I just saw ol' Horace there on the floor and when I realized he was dead, I headed straight for Kate's knowin' you'd be down there for Monday mawnin' breakfast."

"All right, Doc. Stay here. I'm going upstairs." Roman pulled his right hand Colt from its place and slowly ascended the stairs. He stopped after a few steps and turned back toward Doc. "What time did the poker game end last night Doc?"

"Not sure, Rom'. I left early myself, couple'a hands after you did. Maybe… a… midnight."

Roman nodded and continued his climb slowly up the stairs. Three of the four rooms, once occupied by barmaids, were for storage now that the towns populous had dropped notably. Only the room at the end of the hall was used as the couple's bedroom. When Roman reached the landing he went down the long hall to the bedroom and pushed the partially open the door cautiously with his pistol barrel.

"DOC," said Roman from the top of the stairs, "Get up here…QUICK."

Doc was out of breath and could hardly talk when he came into the bedroom. Sheriff Austin was bent down over Roxanne, who was lying on the floor barely alive, her nightclothes soaked in blood. Doc Flagg squatted down beside Roman who had lifted Roxanne's head in his hand. Roman looked at Doc Flagg with inquiring eyes, "Doc?" he said. Doc Flagg only shook his head solemnly.

Roxanne opened her eyes wide when she recognized Roman's voice. "Ro-m-an," she breathed faintly.

"Who did this, Roxanne?" questioned Roman.

Roxanne clutched Roman's coat lapel tight in her fist. "O-oh…Jer-e-miah," she said in a shallow voice as she looked off wistfully. Her response did not seem to be an answer to his question, rather a plea for Jeremiah's presents.

"You mean, Jeremiah Hollinger?" Roman asked.

Fear and pain filled Roxanne's desperate questioning eyes. "ROMAN?" she gasped. She stiffened and expired.

Shaking his head Doc said, "I'm really surprised that kid could do such a thing."

"I'm not so sure he did, Doc," said Roman.

"Doc," said Roman, "You make arrangements to get these two buried proper. Look them over good before you do, see if you can find anything that might help in determining who did this. I'm gonna look around and see if I can find any clues to what happened here last night after we left."

Doc Flagg left and Roman looked around the room for clues. The bed was unmade, but there was no sign of a struggle. Roman went downstairs searching the hallway and the stairs for clues on the way. Other than a few drops of blood, he found nothing that would help him in solving this crime.

Downstairs, Roman found the safe behind the bar open. Apparently, Horace had been counting his daily take when someone came down the stairs and met him at the foot of the stairway. "Robbery wasn't the motive here," thought Roman, "because nothing seems to be missing or out of place."

Roman found a trail of blood droplets from where Horace lay, to the back door and he followed it. Opening the back door he stepped outside onto the porch. Roman brushed his long mustache from side to side with the knuckle of his forefinger as he stood on the step and surveyed the lot behind the saloon. He noticed that the lid on the rain barrel next to the steps on the ground was slightly off center. Curiously, Roman pushed the lid aside and looked down into the barrel. He saw something at the bottom, he focused on the object. It was a knife, a large hunting knife.

Roman stepped down to the ground and removed the lid. Realizing he could not reach all the way to the bottom he tipped the half full barrel and let the water drain out. When it was empty he turned it upside down and dumped the knife out on the ground. Roman picked it up and examined it carefully. Though the knife had been in the water there was still a bloodstain along where the guard and blade came together. This particular knife was very unique. It had a Bowie type blade and a carved ivory handle with the letter 'J' inlaid in silver. Roman knew for sure the owner was Jeremiah Hollinger.

Looking further for some clue, Roman took note of footprints leading away from the steps to the hitching post behind the saloon. There were lots of footprints mixed in the sandy ground, but the ones that were overland on top of the rest were soft soled, with no heel. There was little doubt in Roman's mind to whom these tracks belonged. Pony Davis, was the only one in the area who wore soft-soled buckskin moccasin boots. Pony, a half Black, half-Indian son of a former slave and mountain man and a Navajo Indian woman, lived up in the mountains just above the timberline. Davis got the name Pony, from his skills in catching and taming wild horses. He was a handsome, bronze skinned, dark eyed fellow with long shiny black hair.

Roman and Pony had hunted and fished together for years. Though Roman was twenty years Pony's senior they had become close friends. In fact, the dapple-gray gelding Roman rode had been a gift from Pony. "It just don't make sense," thought Sheriff Austin. "First there's Roxanne's call for Jeremiah and his knife as the murder weapon. Then, there's Pony Davis' foot prints indicating him as the last one to leave the scene of the murder." Roman looked around further to see how someone could get up to the bedroom from outside. The only way possible he figured was for someone to get up on the rain barrel and then climb onto the porch where they would have access to the bedroom window. Trouble was in his haste to get the knife Roman had washed out any tracks that might have been around the barrel.

Roman tried to think it out. "Now if the murderer would have left back through the window, he would've had to come down the stairs after stabbing Roxanne, kill Horace, and then go back upstairs to climb through the window to get outside. No. No," Roman reasoned, "I just don't think it happened that way. Whoever did this went out from downstairs and the blood trail testified to the back door being the exit place."

Roman, Horace, Doc and whoever else wanted to join in would play poker every Sunday night. Roman thought back to the previous night. That particular night, beside himself there had been Horace, Doc, Pony, Jeremiah and Carl the Barber, playing cards.

Jeremiah, who was the son of the biggest rancher around, Clifford P. Hollinger, had lost a bit of money to Horace. Though Jeremiah was upset about losing, Roman didn't think it a motive for him to commit murder. Besides, there was a substantial amount of money left in the open safe.

Jeremiah had left the game, before Roman, after losing a little over fifty dollars. Roxanne complained of a headache fifteen or twenty minutes prior to him leaving and had excused herself to retire for the evening. Next, Roman gave up for the evening. So, that left Pony Davis, Horace, Doc and

Carl the barber. Doc said he left around midnight, so Roman figured Carl the barber would be the next available person to talk with.

When Doc came back with the undertaker and some men to help with the bodies, Roman told him to lock the place up and keep an eye on it. "I surely will," said Doc. Then Roman went off to talk with Carl.

From Carl, Roman learned that he and Pony had left a little after two a.m., Carl remembered the clock striking two. Carl told Roman that Horace had mentioned having a lot of book work to do before he went to bed and would probably be up another hour or two. Carl was beside himself, he could not believe that somebody had killed Horace and his wife.

"Well," Roman thought after his conversation with Carl, "looks like I've got to make a trip out to the Hollinger Ranch. And, probably out to Pony's place too." Having no breakfast and being as hungry as a bear, Roman decided to go back to Kate's and eat first.

Roman took his late morning breakfast in the kitchen at Kate's, he wanted to talk to her about this situation. Roman looked forward to his Monday morning meals at Kate's, she always put on a hardy well-cooked breakfast for him.

"You know, Kate," said Roman as he sopped up the last of his breakfast with a tasty biscuit. "I always considered Roxanne a gold-digger myself, but to have that gal die in my arms like that... that was just plain pitiable. I don't know who this varmint is, but I am darned sure gonna find out.

And, when I do, I'll see to it he hangs for what he has done."

Roman confided in Kate about what he had found at the Lucky Lady Saloon. "I hate to think," he said, "that it was either one of those fellas."

"Well," said Kate as she refilled his coffee cup, "It's no secret that Roxanne slept around with every young fellow that came her way. I don't know about Jeremiah Hollinger, but it was just a few months back that the rumor was she was planning to run off with Pony Davis."

"Dog-gone, Kate," Roman said. "That was just talk. I asked Pony about that myself. He asked me, if I thought he was that stupid, and I said, no, I hardly thought so. He said, 'GOOD'. And, that was that. Just a bunch of old women's gossip."

"Don't sound like a denial to me," said Kate, "And who you callin' old woman?"

"Oh you know what I meant. Anyway, I took it as such," said Roman wanting to defend his friend.

"Suit yourself," Kate said busying herself washing dishes. "But, it sure sounds like he was avoiding the issue to me."

"I suppose you could look at it that way," said Roman. "No matter, I got to be heading out that way after I stop to talk with young Hollinger. I sure don't like this business, but I've got no choice. I intend to get to the bottom of this murder if it's the last thing I do as Sheriff around here."

"You're not going to make that trip now are you? It'll take you 'til midnight to get all the way out to the Hollinger Ranch and then up to Pony's place."

"Ya, you're right about that Kate. Maybe, it would be better if I waited and left early in the morning.

"I'll tell you Kate, this deal makes me want to turn in my badge and give up this job. It just goes against my grain to have to go out and accuse my friends of such a horrible thing. I mean, I'm just getting too old for this kind of headache anyway."

Kate paused from her work and turned toward Roman. She took a breath and with a youthful sparkle in her dark blue eyes, she shook her graying black hair out and let it fall in front of her face across one eye. "We-ll, you know Roman," she said softly with warmth, "I could sell the restaurant. Then, we could get married and move to San Francisco. Jack Doggett has made me a pretty fair offer on the restaurant more than once. He's buying up every piece of loose real estate in town you know."

Roman downed his coffee in a gulp. "Kate," he said ignoring Kate's comment, "How about fixing me a poke of jerky and biscuits for my trip tomorrow?"

The light left Kate's eyes as she dried her hands on her apron. Then she combed her hair back with her fingers. "Sure Roman," she said with a frustrated smile. "I'll have it ready this evening," she said a very matter-of-factly, "Just stop by and pick it up."

"Thanks Kate. You're a queen," said Roman as he slipped his cup into Kate's dishwater and gave her a quick peck on the cheek. "See you later."

"Sure," she said shyly.

Roman stopped at the door and turned. "I like you, Kate. I like you a lot, and there's no one else that I have ever even considered marrying. Well, bye. I'll pick up the poke later."

Halfway to the Hollinger ranch the sun blazed orange and gold from the tops of the mountains; offsetting the sunshine a cool morning breeze blew refreshing and comfortable. Roman enjoyed the desert solitude and admired the green giant Ocotillo with the colorful red blooms at the end. The thought and temptation of Kate's words echoed through his mind. He loved her deeply, much deeper than he cared to admit to himself, but there was no way he would consider marrying her while he had the responsibilities of a lawman. Too many things could go wrong he reasoned in his mind.

As Roman approached the ranch house, Mrs. Hollinger, a tall, gray haired, bold standing woman, came out on the porch with a Henry rifle lying across the crook of her arm. When she recognized Roman she relaxed her stern expression.

"Why, it's you Sheriff. What brings you out this way? Coffee's still hot, come on inside and have a cup."

Respectfully, Roman pulled off his hat. "No, can't today ma'am," he said. "This ain't a social call. I'm conducting an investigating and I need to talk to Jeremiah."

"Jeremiah? Why, him and Cliff are out on the north pasture mending fence with Peg." Peg Johnson was a tough old ranch foreman with a wooden leg, who had worked for the Hollinger's for many years. Peg was a regular poker player too, however he hadn't come to town the night of the murders.

A mothers concern filled Mrs. Hollinger's weathered face. "Jeremiah done somethin' wrong?" she said. "I knew hangin' around them saloons in town was gonna get him into trouble someday."

"I hope Jeremiah's not involved in this, ma'am. Right now, I'm just asking questions. Thank you for the offer of coffee. Maybe, another time." Roman replaced his hat and turned his horse toward the pasture Mrs. Hollinger had mentioned.

It was late morning when the three men stopped their work on a corner post and waited for Roman to ride up. "Sheriff," Clifford Hollinger, a big burly man with a full beard said as a greeting. "What's your business way out here this fine day?"

Roman put his hands on the horn and the back of his saddle lifted and adjusted himself. He leaned forward and faced Jeremiah who had just dipped a ladle of water out of a small barrel setting on the back of a flatbed wagon.

"Horace Pape was killed early morning yesterday at the Lucky Lady Saloon," Roman said directing the statement at Jeremiah face to face.

Noticing the Sheriff was staring straight into his face with hard eyes, Jeremiah took sips of water not losing eye contact over the rim of the ladle and swallowed them slowly. Then he licked his upper lip and threw the rest of the ladle full out across the ground. "Al'm mighty sorry to hear that," he said as he dropped the ladle back into the barrel and wiped his hands on his chaps. "But, what's that got to do with me, Sheriff?"

Maintaining his piercing expression, Roman said, "Where's that fancy Bowie knife of yours Jeremiah?"

With his eyes only, Jeremiah glanced down at where his knife usually hung. He stuttered an answer. "W-ell, I...I don't know. Seems, I lost it somewhere," he said.

"What say," said Roman, "you and me take a little ride and talk about that prize Bowie knife of yours?"

Jeremiah looked over at his father. "Paw? That right with you?" he said.

"I don't see any necessity in you having a private conversation with the Sheriff," said Clifford Hollinger coolly. "I wanna know just what he's a getting' at here. You ain't killed nobody, have ya son?"

"No sir. I shorely ain't." he said.

"I might mention then," said Roman, "that Horace Pape wasn't the only one murdered early the other morning. His wife Roxanne was also killed. Died in my arms as a matter of fact," Roman said with a stiff lip.

Jeremiah's jaw dropped and his eyes swelled wide. "NO... Not Roxanne," he said.

Peg Johnson joined in the conversation reputing sternly. "This boy ain't no murderer," he said.

"Maybe not," said Roman. "But we need to talk, Jeremiah. Now...we can talk here, or we can take that ride. It don't matter which to me, son."

"You been messin' round with that harlot Jeremiah?" said Clifford Hollinger.

"She ain't no harlot Paw," Jeremiah said.
"People juss don't understand her. Yeah Sheriff, I'll take that ride with you now."

Jeremiah went to his horse and swung up into the saddle and the two of them rode slow and when they were a good distance out they held up and Roman turned in his saddle toward Jeremiah.

Roman said, "Was you with Roxanne night before last? And, I want the truth son."

"Yes sir, I was. But, I shore never killed nobody."

"Better tell me the whole story, Jeremiah," Roman said. "You just might be in one heap of trouble, playin' 'round with another man's wife and all."

"I started seein' Roxanne about three months ago" said Jeremiah. "She told me how I could get up to her room by gettin' on the rain barrel and climbin' onto the back porch roof and then through her bedroom window. I been snickin' up there ever' time I come into town. A couple'a weeks ago Roxanne gave me the combination to the safe at the saloon and ever since she's been tryin' to get me to steal Horace's money and run off with her. I told her I couldn't do that, but she's been at me about it ever' time I'm with her."I loved her Sheriff, but I ain't no thief. I can't steal off'n nobody."

"Laying with another man's wife ain't stealing, huh, Jeremiah?" said Roman.

"I reckon I'm guilty shore 'nough there. But, I shore wouldn't kill her, or anyone else for that matter. Unless it was in self-defense a'course," said Jeremiah.

"All right youngin," said Roman, "tell me about the night before last. I aim to tell you here, that Bowie knife of yours is what killed the both of them. You ain't gonna explain that away very easy."

"Well, ain't really much to tell, Sheriff," said Jeremiah. "You were there when Roxanne complained about a headache and went upstairs. That was my signal to pretend to leave and go up to her room. We knew Horace would be playin' cards for quite a spell and then work on his books.

"Before I left, Roxanne tried to get me to rob the safe and run away with her again. When I told her I couldn't do that, she got real upset with me and got so loud I thought she was gonna bring ever'body upstairs. In the rush to leave, I must've dropped my knife and not realized it. When I noticed it was missin', I was hopin' I hadn't lost it there, but I guess maybe I did.

"Sheriff Austin, ain't no more to tell ya 'cept that al'm mighty saddened she's gone. I swear to ya, I never done it. I couldn't kill her. I loved her."

"That's a pretty convincing story, but just the same you ain't off the hook by any means. I hope you've learned a serious lesson from this. You just don't fool 'round with another man's woman. Never."

"Yes sir, Sheriff. I got to agree with that. Darn shame she's dead. I hope you get the man who done it."

"I will," said Roman, "You can bet your life on that. Now, you stay around where I can find you until this is settled. I mean, don't be running off somewhere to buy stock or anything like that. I'll be coming after you if you do. You understand that, don't you son?"

"Yes sir, I shore do," Jeremiah said. "I'll be right out here or in town."

"All right then," said Roman. "You'd better get on back to your fence mending."

"Yes sir, Marshal. Good day to ya," said Jeremiah as he turned his horse and rode back to the fence line. Roman now headed for Pony Davis' place in Blue Rock Canyon.

The sun was low in the afternoon sky when Roman arrived at the cabin; Pony was nowhere around. Roman went inside the cabin and after looking around he came to the conclusion Pony had gone hunting.

Roman went back outside and pulled the saddle off his horse. He put the saddle up on the porch and then tethered his horse in a patch of high grass. Back inside the cabin Roman started a fire in the big stone fireplace. Then he hung the coffeepot and a pot of beans over the fire.

It had just turned dark when Pony came through the door. After hanging his Winchester rifle on the wall he threw a pair of skinned and cleaned rabbits in front of Roman who was sitting at the table.

"What are you doing up here, Roman?" said Pony. "Come up to fish?"

"Nope, not in the mood for fishin'," said Roman. "Been hunting have you?"

"Yeah- yeah… been hunting. Seen ol' Sly Foot out there too. Son-of-a-gun slipped out of my sights again. Went behind a tree just as I was about to get off a shot. That danged old bear's a smart one all right. Mean as they come since that prospector wounded him last year. He's been scratching his mark on the trees pretty close to here lately. I'm figuring I had better get him before he gets me."

"Coffee's hot," Roman said nodding toward the fireplace. "And, I got some beans on the fire that will go good with those cotton tails."

"Yeah. When I saw the smoke I figured it was probably you," said Pony.

"You know," Roman said, "you keep chasing after that old bear and you'll end up like that prospector, chewed up and dead."

"Maybe" said Pony. "But, I'd be a worthy adversary and I'd die fighting.

"Well Roman, if it's not fishing that brings you all this way, what does? I'm sure you didn't come all this way just to talk about my hunting."

"No… No I didn't as a matter of fact," Roman said as his expression turned serious. "But, I figured you could tell me why I'm here."

"How's that?" said Pony with a quiet snicker.

"You know," said Roman, "the thing at the Lucky Lady night before last."

"Something happened?" questioned Pony with curious eyes. "Outside of that Hollinger kid losing a few dollars to Horace, I don't know of anything happening."

"Come on, we have known each other too long for you to try and snow me about something like this. The deal with Roxanne, Pony."

Pony was obviously bothered by Roman's questioning. He said, "Look here Roman, I don't know what you're talking about." Pony avoided eye contact as he carved a rabbit into pieces. "You're talking in circles, it sounds like to me," he said.

"You mean to tell me you didn't spend any time up in Roxanne's bedroom the other night?" said Roman.

"Roxanne's bedroom?" said Pony, now he was really showing his irritation. "Why would I spend any time in Roxanne's bedroom?" Continuing to avoid Roman's accusing stare, Pony slapped pieces of rabbit into a large frying pan. "I played poker that night and I came home. Nothing else happened that I know anything about. And, I thought I had that rumor ended about me and Roxanne here while back."

"I thought so too," Roman said. "But, from the footprints I found in the back of the saloon, you were the last person to leave the place. We found Horace dead and Roxanne dying early the next morning. Thing is, she mentioned a name before she died."

Pony slapped the last piece of rabbit into the pan and went to the fire. He said, "I don't have any idea why that stinking little whore would mention my name."

"I didn't say whose name she mentioned," said Roman. "What makes you call her a whore anyway? And, why are you getting so fired up if you don't know nothing?"

"Come on Roman" said Pony. "Everybody in town knows that woman sleeps around on ol' Horace." Pony wiped his hands on his shirt and searched for his pipe. He found it on a shelf; he tapped it on the shelf to remove old tobacco. Then, he stuffed it full of fresh tobacco that he got off the shelf too.

Roman tipped back in his chair and stuck his thumbs under his gun belt and said, "Not with you, is that what you're saying? You're as innocent as a school boy, right?"

Pony struck a match and lit his pipe. He puffed hard and through the smoke he said, "All right. All right, I saw her a couple of times. But, I didn't kill her… I mean why would I?"

Pony went over and turned the pieces of rabbit in the pan. The aroma of the cooking meat filled the air and calmed the tone of the conversation. Pony knew just the right herbs and spices to bring out the flavor of the meat. Roman was pretty hungry since he hadn't eaten anything but a biscuit and a piece of jerky all day long.

Roman got up and set the table; he knew where everything was though it had been a while since he had been up to the cabin. Little more was said until after the meal was over.

Roman leaned back in his chair and picked his teeth with his small pocketknife. "We-l-l, Pony," he said, "that was one fine meal. But, I got to get back to the subject of those murders at the Lucky Lady Saloon the other night."

Pony jumped to his feet, grabbed the tin plates, and literally threw them into a dishpan. "Look Roman," he said sharply as he turned, "I already told you I didn't do nothing but play cards the other night. Why do you keep bringing that up to me?"

"Because, I think you did it. Or, at least you know something about it," Roman said. "Now, you tell me. I know you were the last person to leave that saloon. And, I figure you dropped what I found in the rain barrel. Now come on, come clean and tell me something here."

Pony quickly grabbed his long hunting knife from its sheath and holding it up, he said, "My knife is right here, Roman."

Roman paused, eyes glistening with angered frustration. Pony stood with his knife in the air. Distinctly Roman said, "Who said it was a knife I found in the rain barrel, Pony?"

"Why... W-why, you did?" said Pony.

"No, Pony I didn't. I hate having to do this my friend, but you're under arrest for the murders of Horace and Roxanne Pape. We'll leave for town in the morning," Roman said. "Now, hand me that knife,."

Pony stood frozen in place with the knife still raised, like a statue of the murderer he was accused of being. Moving nothing but his dark scorching eyes he looked to the Winchester hanging on the wall.

"You don't wanna do that, Pony. I'd have to drop you in your tracks before you got there," said Roman. "I don't wanna shoot a friend, so hand over the knife. I'll see to it you get a fair trial."

"A...A FAIR TRIAL? HA," said Pony. "That's a joke." Then he buried the hunting knife deep into the thick wooden table and collapsed into the chair across from Roman. "There ain't no white-man's court going to give me a fair trial."

"Why did you do it, Pony?" Roman said.

"I didn't say I did anything," said Pony.

"Who did then?" Roman said.

"I don't know nothing," Pony said. "And, I don't wanna talk about it."

"Look here Pony," Roman said, "You're gonna have to talk about it sooner or later. It might as well be now and to a friend."

"I told you," said Pony, "I got nothing to say. If you wanna arrest me and take me in, then, do it. But, I got nothing to say to you."

Roman grabbed the handle of the long hunting knife and struggled to work it out of the table. "Suit yourself then," he said. "Now, I can go get the shackles I brought along and lock you down to the bed for the night. Or, you can give me your word on our friendship that you won't try to run."

"You'd shackle me to the bed like a dog?"

"I'll do whatever necessary to get this thing settled," Roman said. "Now, either give me your word that you won't try to escape or I'll have to shackle you. I don't wanna do that." With that, Roman reared back and threw the long knife and it stuck in the wall just below the rifle.

"All right, I won't," said Pony.

"No, that ain't good enough. I want you to say it," Roman said. "Promise me on your word and our friendship that you won't try to escape on the way back into town."

"Yeah- yeah. You got my word on it. I won't try to escape until we get to town."

Townsfolk came out of shops and saloons to watch from the boardwalks. Others stepped into the street to murmur as Pony rode past with Sheriff Austin close behind. A mother scurried her small children along to get them out of the street and away from the commotion.

Roman took Pony into the jail and put him in one of the two cells. Pony went directly to the window in back of the cell, hopped on a bench, grabbed two fists full of bars and stared silently out toward the mountains where he lived.

Doc Flagg came in as Roman turned the key in the cell door. With a raised brow and questioning eyes he said, "What on earth is goin' on here Rom'? You didn't bring Pony in for those murders did you?"

Roman threw the ring of keys on his desk, unstrapped his gun belt and hung it on a wall hook. "I'm sorry to say, I sure enough did," he said.

"You think Pony did it?" said Doc as he sat down in a chair next to the desk and opened the bottom drawer. He pulled out a bottle of rye whiskey and two glasses. He poured one full and made a questioning gesture with the bottle to Roman.

"Sure, I think he did it," Roman said sharply. "I wouldn't have brought him in otherwise. And yeah, pour. I could use a good stiff drink right now."

Doc filled the second glass and changed the subject nonchalantly as he handed it to Roman. "Hey Rom'," he said after throwing down his drink and making a whistling sound. "What ya gonna do with the Lucky Lady and that forty-five hundred dollars?"

"What?" said Roman with a curious scowl. He threw down his whiskey and tightened his face; normally Roman was a beer drinker. "Woo-wee… that's rough," he said. "I don't know how you can swallow that every day, Doc. Now, just what the heck are you talking about anyway?"

"Ol' Perry Benton told me just this mawnin' that Horace left everything he had to you after Roxanne. Since she's dead, that leaves it all in your hands, Rom'."

Roman sat down in his office chair, leaned back and propped his feet on the desk. "There's got to be a relative somewhere," he said.

"Nope," said Doc. "Benton said, they ain't neither one of'em got a livin' kin he knows of."

"Come to think of it," said Roman, "Horace never talked about any relatives all the time I knew him. Except his mother who died a long time ago.

"We-ll, I don't know what I'd do with a saloon. Forty-five hundred dollars? Whew…," said Roman. "I don't know about that either. I've never seen that kind of money no less had it all at one time."

"Well," said Doc. "You sure enough got it now. You know, I kind'a figgered you'd marry up with Kate and move off somewheres."

"You've got it all figured do you?" said Roman with a note of sarcasm. "I sure am glad you and

Kate got my life all figured out for me. Now, I don't have to do any thinking for myself."

"Aw hell Rom', I don't know who you're tryin' to fool, 'cept'n maybe yourself. You know you love Kate and she loves you. You're just too dad-burn stubborn to admit it, that's all."

Aggravated over the whole day Roman said, "Ain't you got something else to do, Doc?"

Irritated by Roman's comment Doc said, "Yeah, maybe I do. I think I can find a better way to spend my time than fussin' with a stubborn son-of-a-gun like you." With that Doc poured himself a quick shot from the bottle, downed it, then got up and left, slamming the door on his way out.

That evening Roman brought a plate of supper to Pony. He pulled up a chair, sat down beside the cell door and slid the plate under the bars. He said, "Kate sent you a nice plate of steak and potatoes, and a wedge of apple pie."

Pony took the plate and sat on the edge of the bunk . "I ain't really hungry," he said. "But, I guess I'll eat some since Kate sent it. Be sure and thank her for me."

"Sure, I'll be sure and do that. Can we talk a little while you're eating?"

"Well, it ain't like I'm going anywhere. So, you can talk all you want."

"You know, I didn't have any other choice but to bring you in?"

"Sure, I understand that. And, I don't hold it against you; it's always been your job ever sense

I've known you. But, sitting in this jail is driving me crazy. I'd rather be dead than have to sit here."

"I understand," said Roman. "But, if you tell me what you know about the murders of Horace and Roxanne, just maybe I can do something."

"I already told you what I had to say," said Pony with a scowl. "I got nothing more to say on that matter."

"All right, be stubborn then. The Circuit Judge has been sent for and he will be here in a couple of days. I'm trying to save your neck from a noose and you don't want to cooperate. I don't know what's with you, but it's gonna cost you your life if you don't come clean and tell me what you know."

Pony shoved the plate of picked over food across the floor toward Roman and said, "Here, I'm finished. I'll tell you Roman my friend; you do what you have to do, duty and all. But, I got nothing more to say on the matter. I already said, I don't hold it against you. So, unless you're willing to let me out of here, I got nothing to say at all." Pony went and stood on the bench and stared out of the window into the darkness.

Roman was filled with frustration, he didn't know what he could do. He didn't want to see his friend hanged, but at the same time he wanted justice to be served. He wasn't altogether sure Pony committed the murders, though all the evidence pointed in his direction. Pony certainly knew something, but wasn't about to tell it.

Roman mentioned the situation to Kate. She was sympathetic and said she understood he had to do his job, even though Pony was a friend. Doc didn't like the fact that Pony was the accused, but couldn't question Roman's judgment or the evidence at hand either. In fact, when Roman explained what he had found, Doc understood full well why he arrested him. Doc told Roman that from the angle of the stab wounds, he figured they had to be made by a left-handed person. Both Pony and Jeremiah Hollinger were left-handed.

Perry Benton had been practicing law in Bristle Bush ever since the towns beginning and agreed to defend Pony free of charge. Benton had known Pony's father quite well and they were friends, however he couldn't get any answers out of Pony either.

The other lawyer in town was a younger man and had only been around a few months. He was appointed prosecutor for the county and went right to work selecting a jury. He had twelve men picked out in short order; they were miners, shopkeepers and a couple of cowboys.

The evening before the Circuit Judge was to arrive, Roman was sitting at his desk making notes and evaluating the evidence he had concerning the murders. He listed Roxanne calling Jeremiah's name, the blood trail leading to the back door, the knife in the rain barrel, the moccasin footprints in the back lot and the most disturbing of all, Pony's continued silence.

Roman shook his head hopelessly and laid down his pen. As he leaned back in his chair he heard a commotion coming from outside. He got up from his seat just as a large rock came crashing through the front window of the jail. Roman looked out and saw a crowd of vigilantes made up of fifteen to twenty miners and cowboys. Some carried torches and pick handles, a few were toting rifles or shotguns. Many were packing six-shooters besides the other weapons.

"What's going on out there, Roman?" said Pony from the cell door.

"Looks like a few of the folks around here want to mete out a little justice of their own," Roman said. "But, don't worry, you're my prisoner. Ain't nobody gonna do anything as long as you're under my care."

"Give me a rifle," said Pony. "I'll go out and face them myself. It'll be better than hanging. I'll go down fighting."

"I can't do that and you know it. Now, sit down and be still," said Roman. "I'll handle this."

Roman was strapping on his pistols when someone outside yelled. "Send that murderer out here to face his judgment. Or, we will come in and get him."

Roman recognized the voice. It was Big Jim Bell, a wide shouldered giant of a man that stood near seven feet tall. He was a mine foreman that everybody had respect for as a brawler. Roman did not look forward to facing him on opposing sides; he knew he would have to be cool and show resolute force.

Roman stepped outside and closed the door quickly behind him and faced the crowd. Standing on the porch put Roman eye to eye with Big Jim. Jeremiah Hollinger stood beside Big Jim; his left hand on his six-gun and a rope in his other.

Roman wrapped his hands around both Colts at his sides and addressed Big Jim straight on. "Well Jim," Roman said. "I take it you're the leader of this bunch?"

"That is right, sure I am. We do not intend to let some Judge let the murderer of that sweet, pretty little girl get off without his judgment. We are here to see to it he is hanged by his neck for what he has done."

The mob shook their heads in agreement and responded with mumblings of 'hanging'. Roman could smell the odor of cigar smoke and whiskey emanating from the crowd. It was obvious that strong drink was the force motivating this lynch-mob.

"You know, Jeremiah," Roman said with a raised brow. "I haven't completely ruled you out as a suspect in this yet. That's why I told you to stick around where I could find you. I mean, your knife was the murder weapon." Some in the crowd began to speak in whispers among themselves, as they looked Jeremiah's way.

"You know I loved her, Sheriff. I would never bring no harm to her," said Jeremiah.

"Oh-h, I don't know about that, Jeremiah. Jealousy has caused many a man to do things he wouldn't ordinarily do. After all everyone knows about Roxanne and Pony. Did it finally get to you Jeremiah?"

All eyes were on Jeremiah now. "He... He's just tryin' to save his friend," Jeremiah said. "He knows who done the killin', and it weren't me. I loved Roxanne."

"I am sure the truth is going to come out in the trial," Roman said. "Jim, I want you to break this crowd up right now. Just go on back home and let the law handle this matter. I won't allow a lynching as long as I'm the Sheriff."

"Don't listen to 'em Big Jim," said Jeremiah. "We can take 'em and hang that murderin' Indian." Jeremiah was quite bold with whiskey doing his talking and a crowd behind him.

No sooner had Jeremiah got the words out of his mouth than Roman had both Colts drawn. One pointed at Big Jim's nose and the other against Jeremiah's chest. "I said break this up and go home," said Roman forcefully.

"Why, I'l..," is all that Big Jim got out of his mouth when Roman rapped his forehead hard with his pistol barrel. Jim dropped to his knees dazed and moaning. He held his bleeding forehead in his hands. Roman cocked both pistols and still pointing at Jeremiah's chest and Big Jim's head he said, "I ain't used to chewing my words twice. I said break this up or I'll charge the whole lot of you with disorderly conduct and obstructing justice. Now-MOVE OUT."

With Big Jim out of commission the crowd lost their backbone and started to break up muttering as they slowly walked away. A couple of men helped Big Jim to his feet and they headed toward a nearby saloon. However Jeremiah held his ground.

"I aim to see Pony Davis hanged for murderin' Roxanne," Jeremiah said. "You know he did it, Sheriff. An', I won't let ya get him off jess cause he's yer friend, if I have to kill him myself."

"Don't you buck me boy," said Roman. "The law will handle this. If you interfere with my job again, I'll put a hole in your chest big enough to drive a freight wagon through." Roman shoved the pistol barrel into Jeremiah's chest. "Now get on outta here before I forget that I'm a lawman."

Reluctantly, Jeremiah turned and started off with the few stragglers left of the crowd. After about five paces he stopped and turned. He glared at Roman as he rubbed his chest where he had been poked with the pistol barrel.

"I said, GET," Roman said. Jeremiah hung his head and went to the saloon with others.

The trial took only one day from start to finish. To Roman's displeasure his testimony was the most damning. Jeremiah's testimony was nearly word for word what he had told Roman out on the range. Doc didn't have a lot to say outside of testifying that he had played cards that night and that the murderer was more than likely left handed.

Though Perry Benton made a noble effort to emphasize Pony's good character and put up a defense, he had little success, especially since Pony chose to remain silent through the whole trial. Pony would only sit and stare out of the window of the courthouse toward the mountains.

The jury took less than two hours to bring in a verdict. Peg Johnson, the Hollinger's ranch-hand, had been appointed jury foreman. Roman strongly objected to the appointment, but had proved unsuccessful. Peg read the verdict to the judge. "We the Jury unanimously find the defendant, guilty as charged."

Peg addressed Pony personally, "Sorry, Pony. It was a hard decision, but the evidence says ya did it." Pony gave him a brief glance of recognition and returned to staring out the window.

The courtroom roared with chatter and calls of, "Hang him. Hang him high." A couple of sympathizers who liked Pony reputed those doing the yelling and there was shoving and name calling. The judge had to pound his gavel repeatedly and threaten to hold the whole crowd in contempt. Roman had to assure he would enforce the judge's order before the crowd would quiet down.

Then, as everyone expected, the judge sentenced Pony to hang on the following Saturday morning. With shackles on his feet and hands, Pony stood staring out of the window as the judge pronounced sentence. When asked if he had anything to say to the court, he only maintained silence.

The judge left town the next day. Roman was in a terribly foul mood after the trial. He even got in a fuss with Kate over nothing, and Doc would hardly speak to him he was so cross.

The pounding of construction work on the gallows awakened Roman early Friday morning. He cursed as he dressed and got ready to go for breakfast.

Roman stepped outside and strapped on his Colts and adjusted his gun belt. Then he stretched as he looked up and down the street; something he had done most every morning for the last eleven years.

He contemplated, "Maybe it's time to give this up?" Roman cleared his mind of thinking about that and stepped down off the boardwalk. The streets were deserted except for a scraggly scavenger dog searching for scraps, and the two men contracted to build the gallows.

Roman walked down the street and crossed over to Kate's to pick up breakfast for himself and Pony. He grabbed up the basket of food and left quickly, he didn't want to get into a conversation with Kate and he didn't want to leave his prisoner unattended for long.

Pony was sitting on the edge of his bunk when Roman returned. Roman hung his gun belt up and went over to the cell. He slid the plate under the bars as usual; he noticed that Pony had a strange look on his face.

"What's with you today?" said Roman.

"Nothing," said Pony calmly.

"Then why do you have that cockeyed smile on your face?" Roman said.

Pony shook his head, then paused. "I did it you know," he said.

"What… What did you say?" Roman said.

Pony's dark eyes were serious as death itself. "I said, I did it," he said. "I killed Roxanne and Horace."

Roman sat the basket of food down on his desk and pulled his chair up to the cell door.

"Why Pony?" said Roman. "What reason on earth would you have to kill them?"

"You know that rumor you ask me about awhile back," said Pony. "It was true. I'd been seeing Roxanne for quite some time. She kept hounding me to steal Horace's money and run off with her to California. I refused. I tried to stay away from her, but I just couldn't.

"I asked her if that was all she wanted out of me. She said no, that she really loved me. She said nobody had ever made her feel the way I made her feel. I believed her, Roman," said Pony. "I really believed her." Pony paused, his eyes glassed over with deep hurt.

Pony voice quivered a little as he continued, "I…I hadn't been with her for a while and I knew Horace was going to be up late doing his bookwork down stairs, so I climbed up to her room from the porch roof as usual. Roxanne seemed upset about something and wouldn't talk to me about it. She said she didn't want me coming around, that she didn't care for me anymore. I asked her how that could be. She just laughed. I asked her if there was someone else. She only laughed again and said, 'There were a number of someone elses'.

"How could that be? I felt uncontrollably angry. That's when I saw Jeremiah's hunting knife lying on the floor beside the bed. I asked, 'what's this?' as I picked it up; I knew who it belonged to. She said it belonged to the man that was going to take her away from there and to a better life. I said, 'MAN? Ha, Jeremiah Hollinger is just a kid'. I don't remember much of what happened next. I was so angry. I remember…I remember plunging that knife deep into her.

"Next, I found myself walking down the stairs, I still had that bloody knife in my hand. When I was near the bottom, Horace heard me and turned from in front of the safe. He had a curious look on his face. Then he saw the knife. He said something; I don't remember what it was. Then he started for me screaming Roxanne's name. I caught him at the bottom of the stairs and I must have stabbed him too. Everything's pretty foggy after that. I remember sliding the lid back on the rain barrel and dropping the knife in it. Then... I got on my horse and rode. The next thing I remember is being at home."

Astounded at Pony's confession, Roman said, "I can hardly believe this, Pony. I'm gonna send one of my closest friends to the gallows for killing another one of my friends." Roman shook his head. "Why didn't you tell me before now? Maybe, I could have said something to the judge and got you a prison sentence instead of a hanging."

"I couldn't spend any time in prison. And, I'm not going to hang, Roman," said Pony.

Curiously Roman said, "Yes, I'm sorry to say you are gonna hang for those murders."

With that, Pony pulled out from under the blanket on the end of the bed a .38 caliber Double-Action Colt that Roman kept in the bottom drawer of the desk with Doc's whiskey.

"No Roman, I won't be hanged," said Pony. "I cannot be locked up in a prison either. I've got to be free to fight. I don't mind dying for what I did, but I have to die fighting."

"How...What?" said Roman. He looked toward the desk.

"That's a bad habit you've got of leaving your keys on the desk, Roman," said Pony. He held the keys up in his other hand and jingled them at Roman. "I pulled some of the rope webbing out of the bed and lassoed the keys."

Pony stood up with the pistol trained on Roman and opened the unlocked cell door and stepped out.

"Now, old friend," said Pony. He pointed with the pistol, "Inside."

"You don't wanna do this, Pony," said Roman. "You promised me you wouldn't try to escape."

"No," said Pony. "I promised I wouldn't try to escape until I got to town. Now, get in there before I have to shoot you."

"You won't shoot me," said Roman.

"No, I wouldn't kill you," Pony said. "But, I'd sure enough cripple you if you don't get in that cell right now."

Roman knew Pony meant what he said, so reluctantly he went inside. Pony slammed the door shut and locked it behind him. Then he threw the keys in the corner of the other cell.

As Pony got to the door Roman said, "PONY." Pony turned as he opened the door. The two men locked eyes. "I'll be coming after you. You know I will?"

"I know," said Pony. "You gotta do what you gotta do. And, I gotta do what I gotta do." Pony turned and dashed out the door.

Roman went to the cell window and yelled out hoping one of the men working on the gallows would hear him. He heard a horse galloping out of town toward the mountains.

A few moments later Doc came rushing through the front door. "ROM'," he said, then he saw Roman in the cell. "What the hell?"

"Get the keys in the other cell over there and get me out of here," said Roman pointing. "HURRY."

Doc went to the second cell and found the keys. As he unlocked the cell door Doc said, "Pony stole a horse from in front of the general store and rode hell-bent out of town. I'll start roundin' up men for a posse."

"NO. Don't do that. I need to handle this alone," said Roman as he strapped on his gun belt and pulled a Winchester rifle out of the wall rack.

"You won't be any match for that half-breed up in those mountains," said Doc. "You'd better take some men along."

Roman grabbed a box of cartridges and said, "I will handle this alone I said."

"Suit yourself. Darn, you're a stubborn man," Doc said.

"I'm going down and get my horse," said Roman. "Doc, don't you let anybody come up there; I'll bring him back. And, listen." Roman paused. "If something should happen to me, tell Kate I love her. Okay?"

"Like I could stop anybody," said Doc. "You're a darn..."

"OKAY, Doc?" said Roman, "Look, I'm counting on you."

"All right. All right, you know I'll do my best," assured Doc. "You be careful. Don't take no unnecessary chances, ya hear? You tell Kate yourself when ya get back."

Pony had a good half hour start on Roman and it took two hours of serious riding to get to Pony's cabin. Of course this was no problem for Roman's dapple-gray; Pony had given him an excellent mount.

Roman left his horse in the trees away from the cabin when he arrived. With rifle ready he eased up to the cabin. The horse Pony had taken from town was stripped of saddle and gear and was tethered out in the grass. Roman stepped lightly on the porch and peeked inside through the window. The cabin looked deserted from outside, nevertheless, Roman used caution opening the door and going inside.

Roman's .38 caliber Colt was lying on the table. Other than that, everything seemed as they had left it. Even Pony's rifle was still on the wall. Roman walked around inside the cabin looking for some clue that would tell him where Pony might be. Then it came to him. He had stuck Pony's long knife in the wall just below the rifle. Roman turned quickly and looked at the spot where the knife should be. Only a narrow slit of a hole in the wood testified to it having been there. The knife was gone. Roman ran back to his horse and swung up. He held his rifle across the front of his saddle and headed into the tall, fragrant pines.

As Roman rode deeper into the trees he noticed the claw marks Pony had mentioned on a couple of trees where Sly Foot had scratched deep into the bark marking territory. "Surely," Roman said to himself, "Pony wouldn't go up against that bear with nothing but a knife." However, Roman knew good and well, yes he would.

A little farther into the forest Roman spotted what appeared to be fresh bear tracks and held up. He dismounted to take a closer look and as he bent down he saw alongside the tracks those familiar moccasin impressions that belonged to no one else but Pony. "Yes. Yes he would at that," Roman said out loud as looked up from the tracks. As Roman stood up he heard a commotion. It sounded like growling and yelling coming from a clearing a few hundred yards away. He quickly mounted his horse again and hurried toward the sounds.

Roman broke out of the trees into the clearing and saw, down in a little valley, in waist high grass, a life and death struggle. Pony and a large black bear that, towered over him, were locked in each other's deadly grasp. Pony plunged his long hunting knife into the bear's side again and again. However, it seemed to have little effect against the large beast's aggressive attack.

Roman steadied his horse and shouldered his Winchester. He took careful aim at Sly Foot's huge head. Just as he was about to squeeze off his shot the bear and Pony fell into the tall grass where Roman couldn't see them.

Roman lowered his rifle and kicked his horse into a gallop across the clearing and down into the tall grass where the bear and Pony were. When Roman got there the great black creature lay still and silent on top of Pony. Roman swung his leg over and jumped from his saddle hitting the ground running toward Pony who was almost completely covered by the motionless body of the big black bear.

Roman yelled Pony's name. He struggled to roll the massive carcass off of his friend. After much effort Roman manage to get the bear off of Pony who was barely alive and breathing laboriously. Pony's long knife was sunk deep into the broad chest of the bear. Apparently the long blade had hit the bear's heart and killed him instantly, but not before he had time to do mortal damage to his foe. Roman realized Pony was brief moments away from death.

Roman knelt down beside his friend and lifted his head in his hand. Pony was covered in blood head to foot, some of the bear's, but mostly his own. There were large gaping wounds that shone through his ripped clothing in numerous places in his flesh.

"That was a damned fool thing to do. Go up against a bear that size with just a knife," said Roman as he shook his head. "You're not Davy Crockett, you know?"

Pony struggled to talk and said, "Like…I said. You had to do what you had to do. And…and, I had to do…what I had to do. I wasn't going to hang. I had to go out fighting."

"Hold on there friend" said Roman. "I'll get you some water." Roman laid Pony's head in the grass very gently and went to his horse and got his canteen.

He returned to Pony, lifted his head and poured a small amount of water into Pony's mouth.

"Tha...thanks," Pony said weakly. "I beat that bear. Didn't I?"

"You sure did," said Roman. "Yes you did.

Pony said in barely more than a whisper, "It had to be this way, Roman. I couldn't let you hang me."

"I know," said Roman holding back his emotions.

"I beat that bear," Pony said again. Then he choked, blood ran from the corner of his mouth. Eyes glassy and expressionless, he died in Roman's arms. Roman sat rocking his friend, looking far off for a long while. "Yes you did, Pony. Yes you did," he repeatedly said. A lone tear rolled down his cheek and dropped off his chin, despite his struggle to hold it back.

Roman buried Pony behind the cabin and hung the bear's claws on a grave marker he made for him. It was a long solemn ride back to Bristle Bush, and Roman had a lot of time to think about what he was going to do with the rest of his life. It was late afternoon when Roman got back into town.

After he stabled his horse, Roman stopped at the mayor's house briefly. Then he went to his office, washed up, put on his best suit of clothes and polished his boots.

Roman was on his way to lawyer Benton's office when he met Doc on the street just as he was about to step inside. "I knew you were back," said Doc, "I saw your horse down at the livery. What happened up there? Where's Pony?" Roman told

Doc the whole story and he just shook his head as Roman finished it.

"Well, ain't that somethin'," Doc said. "I wasn't lookin' forward to seein' him hang no-ways. He was prob'ly right. It was a better way for him to die than bein' hanged. Fought and killed a bear with just a knife. Boy, ain't that somethin'."

Then Doc pulled a cigar out of his breast pocket and struck a match on the side of the building. He talked around the cigar as he lit it and puffed hard to get it going. "Where ya goin' all spit and shined anyway?" asked Doc.

"Doc," Roman said, "Go on over to Grady Tucker's Saloon and I'll be there shortly. Tell you what, I'll buy you a drink of good whiskey."

"What're gonna do, Rom'?" questioned Doc.

"I'll explain later," said Roman. "Now, go on over there. I'll be along shortly."

Doc agreed and headed for the saloon.

Roman was in Benton's office for a half-hour or so. Next, he stopped at the stage line office and after that, he went straight to Grady Tucker's Saloon. There he ordered up a double shot of the best whiskey Grady had for Doc and a beer for himself. Doc kept questioning him about what he was doing, but Roman wouldn't give him any answers.

Doc threw down three drinks; two double shots of Imported whiskey that Roman bought for him and one rye that he bought for himself. Roman drank two beers and as Doc lit his cigar for the fourth or fifth time he said, "Come on, Doc. You'll wanna see this."

"See what?" said Doc. "What's goin' on here, Rom'? Where we goin'?"

"Just come on with me," Roman said. "I'm going down to see Kate."

"This time of day? Are ya nuts? That Friday supper crowd will be in nere, an' she'll be a cookin' up a storm to keep up with that hungry bunch."

"Oh, quit complaining, Doc, and come on," Roman said.

It was just as Doc had described it. The place was packed with customers and all of Kate's extra help was rushing back and forth to and from the kitchen. Rather than fight his way through the crowd Roman went outside and around to the back where the kitchens door was open. He went inside with Doc right behind him. Kate was so busy cooking and getting out orders that she didn't notice Roman and Doc come in.

"KATE," said Roman over all the kitchen noise.

She looked up from the stove, hair in her face and beads of sweat running down her cheeks. "Roman?" she said. "When did you get back? I'm glad to see you're safe, but I can't talk right now. As you can see, I'm pretty busy. Glad you're back." Kate went back to her work.

"KATE," said Roman again. "I've got to talk to you. NOW."

"What…Now? Roman, I'm really busy tryin' to cook for that hungry mob I got out there."

"Now, Kate," said Roman insistently. "I gotta talk, now."

"What? What on earth can be that important?" asked Kate. She saw in Roman's eyes an excited spark she didn't remember ever seen before. "Oh… All right," she said. "I hope this is really important." Kate handed the cooking utensils to one of her helpers. Then she wiped her face and hands with her apron as she came over to the door where Roman and Doc stood.

Roman nodded and smiled. "Come on, outside Kate," he said.

"Outside?" she said. "What? Ro-man?"

Roman grabbed Kate gently by the hand and led her outside. "Kate," Roman said as he looked deep into her questioning eyes, "I think it's about time I let you know just how much I love you. And, if you're still willing, I'd like you to marry me. I've made a deal through Perry Benton to sell the Lucky Lady to Jack Doggett. He also said Doggett would still be interested in buying the restaurant. So, what do say, Kate? We'll move to California."

"You know I will, Roman," said Kate. She grabbed Roman around the neck and hugged him tight. Roman bent forward and kissed her long and passionately.

"I'll be," said Doc. "It certainly is about time you two got together for keeps."

Kate pushed away from Roman and with a questioning look she said, "Roman, what about your job as Sheriff? And, what happened with Pony?"

"W-ell Kate," Roman said. "Pony's gone Kate. I'll fill you in on the details later. As for being Sheriff I'll be forty-eight years old this month. I figure I better quit while I'm ahead. I turned in my resignation and badge to the mayor when I got back in town this afternoon."

"Oh-h Roman, I love you," said Kate as she hugged his neck again.

Roman pulled some contracts out of his breast pocket and opened one. "Here Kate, sign this and it will all be taken care of."

"Here? Now?" said Kate.

"Sure," said Roman. "Unless you really don't want to marry me and go to California."

"Oh, I want to" said Kate. "But, I don't have a pen and ink. Wait, I got one inside. I'll be right back. And, don't you go nowhere."

As Kate opened the door Roman said, "Hey Kate."

"What?" Kate said as she turned back to see Roman waving something at her. "What's that?"

"Tickets to San Francisco," Roman said.

"Roman," Kate said, "you've made me a very happy woman."

"You've made me happy, Kate," said Roman. "You just get these papers signed so I can get them back to Benton."

"All right," she said. Kate went inside and got a pen and ink.

"I don't have anything to write on," Kate said when she returned.

"Here, use this," said Doc bending and offering his back.

THE END

A DEADLY PRESUMPTION

Tommy Bowling was in Pete's Place when the stranger came in. Tommy pulled a crumpled piece of paper out of his shirt pocket, looked at it, and then got in such a hurry that he stumbled and tripped over his own feet leaving the saloon. He just could not get on his horse fast enough to ride out to the Cord ranch and tell Phinehas.

Now according to some eastern newspaper clippings and a dime novel, Ed Gant had killed nearly thirty men. Half that many would have been closer to the truth, and most of that figure was in a Texas range war. Gant had a reputation as a gunfighter sure enough, and he had put down his share of notorious shootists. Always a fair fight though; they said he never drew first.

Phinehas Cord was sitting on the corral fence watching his young fiancée Leah exercise a new mare he had bought for her in Tucson when Tommy came racing down the road and stormed into the lot. Tommy reined back and slid his horse to a halt in a cloud of dust in front of the corral.

Tommy's horse wasn't fully back on its feet before Tommy was clambering at Phin who had jumped down from the fence. Eyes wide and jumping with excitement he said, "It's HIM. It's HIM. He's in Martin's Break right now, at Pete's Place."

"It's who?" said Phin as he grabbed Tommy by the shoulders. "Calm down here and talk to me a minute, dog-gone it. Who's in Martin's Break at Pete's?"

"HIM," said Tommy as he shoved the worn newspaper clipping into Phin's face that he had just pulled out of his shirt.

Phin snatched the paper from Tommy, stepped back and looked at it. "Ed Gant's in Martin's Break?" said Phin. "You sure it's Ed Gant, Tommy? What would he be doin' in Martin's Break anyhow?"

"Don't know fer shore. Told Pete he was waitin' for someone," said Tommy.

"How do you know it's him for sure?" Phin said. "Did he say so?"

"It's him I tell ya. Said his name was Gant. Looks just like that ther pitch'r. Phin, yer goin' in ain't ya? Ed Gant's killed near thirty men."

"Ed Gant huh," said Phin, his blue eyes smiled with anticipation. "Yeah, you bet I'm goin' in. Gant's just what I've been waitin' for. I'll wash up and get my pistols.

"Tommy," said Phin, "you go back into Martin's Break and make sure Gant stays put until I get there."

"You bet'cha, Phin. I'll keep him around if I have to buff'lo him myself."

Leah approached the corral gate and asked, "What is going on, Phin? What is Tommy so excited about?"

"Nothin' you should concern yourself with darlin'," said Phin. "You just go ahead and enjoy that mare. I got to get cleaned up and go into

Martin's Break to take care of some business. Don't you worry, I'll be back in time for supper."

"I'll put the mare up and go with you," Leah said.

"NO," said Phin sharply. "N-o. You need to stay here and wait on your parents. I'll be back before supper. This is man's business and it ain't a woman's concern." Phin turned and hurried toward the house.

Inside, he hurriedly stripped off his shirt and poured a pan of water. He told his Mexican housekeeper to get him a clean shirt.

He was washed down to his waist and jamming a clean shirt into his britches when Leah came into the house. Phin paid her little mind as he removed a holstered pair of nickel plated Colts from off the wall rack and buckled them around his waist. Leah stood silent as Phin loaded the two pistols with new cartridges from a drawer in the gun case. One at a time Phin spun the cylinders on his arm and held the pistols up to his ears. Listening intently he smiled at the precision sound of the movements. Phin clicked the hammers, spun both pistol in his hands and planted them firmly in place one at each side.

Leah took a deep breath and crossed her arms. Her almost black, dark brown eyes were flashing with frustration. "You are going into Martin's Break to start a gun fight aren't you?" she said.

"What if I am?" said Phin. "I told you it ain't nothin' for you to be concerned about. I'll get this taken care of quickly and be back here before your parents even get here."

"If you are still alive you mean," Leah said as tears welled up in her eyes. "Ed Gant is a seasoned killer, Phin. He's not a half drunk cowboy or a young inexperienced man like Jimmy Rowe, that you can goad into a fight."

"Yeah, what about Jimmy Rowe?" said Phin. "I know you were sweet on him. He should have known better than draw down on me."

"I never had anything for Jimmy and you know it Phin," Leah said. "He just liked to talk, that's all. He was a nice boy."

Tears of frustrated emotion welled up in Leah's heart and she felt a lump in her throat as she started to speak. "Oh-h Phin," she said, "I just... I just don't understand you at all sometimes. Why do you do this to me?"

"I ain't doin' nothin' to nobody," said Phin. "I told you before, my mother died out here on this ranch and no one even knew it. A year and a half ago the old man died and if it wasn't for this ranch, no one would have known he ever lived. People are going to know who Phin Cord is. When I walk down the street with my woman at my arm, people are gonna step aside, because they'll know who I am and what my reputation is. They'll have respect."

"You don't have to kill someone to have respect," Leah said tearfully trying to reason with Phin. "Just treat people right."

"My old man was good to people and all anyone ever done was take advantage of him. Nobody, is gonna take advantage of me. Never."

"Please Phin, don't go," Leah said. "Ed Gant will kill you."

"Don't you worry about that my dear. I'm the fastest there is. Nobody can beat me. You'll see, I'll be back in time for supper."

"Phin," Leah said firmly as she straightened herself and dried her tears with a hanky. "I won't take this anymore, if and when you come back I won't be here. I mean it, Phin."

"Suite yourself," said Phin. "But, I'll be back and you'll come back too. You're my woman and we're gonna get married soon."

"Not this time, Phin. This is it, I won't see you anymore. I have had enough of gun fighting and killing."

Phin tightened his lips and made fists with his hands, his eyes were fiery with rage. He turned and stormed out of the house slamming the door behind him with all his angry force.

In Martin's Break, Tommy was at the head of the bar talking to Pete the saloon owner and watching the stranger playing poker with two local cowboys. Pete removed a black stub of a cigar he was chewing on from his teeth and pointed at the stranger with the chewed end. "You know," he said, "I thought I heard that Ed Gant had a scar in his upper lip from bein' smacked with a gun butt?"

"Hell Pete," said Tommy. "How could you see it under that big thick mustache?"

"Oh…Yeah," said Pete. "Prob'ly why he's got a mustache, huh?" Pete stared at the stranger curiously.

Phin Cord entered the saloon and paused in the doorway. He studied the men playing cards, they paid him little attention. Then he walked over to the bar where Pete and Tommy were standing. "Is that him over there?" asked Phin.

"Yeah, the one against the wall to McCann's right," said Tommy.

Pete scratched his scruffy beard and brushed his bushy mustache with his finger and pointed with the cigar again. "You know," he said. "I don't think he's got no scar 'neath that mustache, Tommy."

Phin looked at Tommy and said, "What the hell's he talkin' about?"

"Will ya shut up about the damned scar, Pete," said Tommy. "Pro'bly just a damned story anyway. I tell ya, that's shore enough Ed Gant. Look at the dog-gone picture."

Tommy slapped the old worn newspaper clipping on the bar. Pete looked at it and then at the stranger playing poker. "Yup," he said. "It does look like'm- sorta?"

Phin looked hard at Tommy. "You're sure about this Tommy?" he said.

"Al'm damned shore, Phin," said Tommy. "Hell, fer shore his names Gant, an' he looks just like that there pitch'r don't he?"

Phin raised his palm to silence the pair and started to ease his way down the bar. He stopped and stood watching the stranger play cards from about eight feet away. The men playing cards did not seem to be bothered by his presence. After a few minutes Phin flexed his fingers and stood erect and loose.

Suddenly "GANT," said Phin. Through squinted eyes the stranger peered across the dim lit room at this challenging figure.

"That's right," said Phin sharply. "I'm talkin' to you mister. Your names Gant, ain't it?"

"Yeah, I'm Gant," said the stranger. "Don't think I know you though."

"Stand up Gant," Phin said. "Face, Phinehas J. Cord."

"What for kid? I don't know you," Gant said.

"I know you, Gant. And, I'm sayin' you're a yellow dog card cheat. I saw you slip that last card out of your vest pocket," said Phin.

"Hey, what's this about, kid? I ain't no card cheat, and I ain't slipped no cards. What's your beef son."

"I ain't no son of yours. I said you're a low down card cheat. Now, either admit to it or stand up and draw that hog-leg you got there."

Gant's anger was up now. He stood up and kicked his chair aside. The other two card players got up and moved quickly out of the way.

"Look kid," said Gant, "I don't know what your problem is but, you're sure enough getting' under my skin."

"Too bad. Go for that smoke-wagon if you don't like it," said Phin.

"I won't draw on you kid," Gant said.

"TOMMY," said Phin. "Give us a count to three. On three Gant."

Gant said, "I ain't drawin' on you kid. Forget it."

"I'm drawin' on you on the three count," Phin said. "Either way Gant, you're a dead man."

Without taking his eyes off of his prey Phin said, "TOMMY Count."

"All…all right Phin," Tommy said, his eyes jumped with excitement as he began the count. "One…Two…Three..."

Gant hesitated a brief moment and Phin waited for him to make a move. When he did make his move; in a flash Phin drew both Colts and **-BOOM-** two deafening explosions from Phin's pistols sent Gant sprawling backward against the wall to his instant death.

Phin let out the breath he had been holding and slowly a grin filled his face. With a twinkle in his eye he chuckled and said, "Did you see that? I beat Ed Gant, I beat him bad. He hardly even cleared leather. I told you boys, I'm the fastest there is. Nobody can beat me."

Dave McCann, one of the poker players spoke up. "Somebody will come along," he said. "And, it might be sooner than you think."

"You want to try your luck, McCann?" said Phin.

"No, not me," said McCann. "I ain't no gunman."

"Good. Then carry that sorry son-of-a-gun out of here," said Phin.

"TOMMY," called Phin.

"Yeah Phin," called back Tommy obediently.

"Help McCann get this dead body out of here," Phin ordered and then said, "Drinks on me for everybody when you get back."

"You bet'cha Phin," Tommy said enthusiastically.

Tommy and McCann picked up the lifeless body and started toward the door. "Here take this too," said Phin as he picked the stranger's hat up off the floor. Phin noticed something, the initials C J G burned into the band. "What's this mean?" he wondered. He shrugged and tossed the hat on the corpse.

Tommy and McCann awkwardly carried the dead man out of the saloon.

They were back within fifteen minutes. McCann collected his drink and went back to the table to sit by himself. Everyone else took their drinks at the bar with Phin.

Shortly, another stranger walked through the saloon doors at Pete's Place. He addressed the small group and said, "Afternoon men. I'm supposed to meet my brother here. His horse is outside, but I don't see him around. You fellas seen him by any chance?"

The saloon was silent. Phin took note of the stranger. He noticed the newcomer had a scar running from the corner of his top lip and almost to his nose.

"What's your business here, stranger?" said Phin.

"Like I said, I'm supposed to meet my brother here. He goes by C J, C J Gant. I'm the new appointed U.S. Marshal, and my brother's comin' down to join me and be my deputy."

The stranger pulled back his vest to reveal a U.S. Marshals star pinned to his shirt. Then his eyes narrowed and turned real serious. He addressed the men in the saloon again. "I have the feelin' you boys know somethin' about my brother," he said.

Tommy, not being able to contain himself any longer spoke up proudly and said, "Yeah- we shore do. In fact we just carried him out'a here. Phin there out gunned him in a fair fight."

Phin turned to face the stranger and took a step back away from the bar. "You're Ed Gant, ain't you mister?" he said.

"That's right," said Ed Gant. "You the one gunned down my brother?"

"Yeah," said Phin. "As a matter-a-fact I am. He was cheatin' at poker and I called him on it."

"I find that hard to be true. I don't believe that for a minute. C J never learned poker."

"That's right," said McCann from the table. "We were teachin' him when young Phin there goaded him into a fight by accusin' him of cheatin'. He wasn't cheatin', cause he didn't know hardly nothin' about playin'."

With a cold hard glare and a demanding tenor Marshal Ed Gant said, "So you think you're a pistoleer, huh sonny? Hand over them fancy pistols youngster. I'm arrestin' you for the murder of my brother a U.S. Deputy Marshall."

"I...I ain't gonna hand you nothin'" said Phin. "You know, I out-drew your brother and I'll out-draw you too." Phin took a step back and readied himself, but this time his confidence was shaken; yet his pride couldn't and wouldn't let him give it up.

"If that's the way you want it, sonny," said Marshal Gant. "Then I reckon I can sure enough oblige you."

Gant stood firm. Phin went for his right hand Colt. He beat Marshal Gant's draw by a measure, but he was not as sure of himself as before. Phin's shot took off Gant's hat and skimmed his hair. However, when Gant's .44 spoke the slug was true; young Phin fell and lay on the floor lifeless.

As McCann stepped over him and was leaving he said, "Told ya."

A stiff breeze blows on a lonely hill a few hundred yards behind the deteriorated Cord ranch house. The stout wind clears dust off of one of the three grave markers. Washed out and barely visible the words appeared-

PHINEHAS J. CORD
SHOT BY MARSHAL ED GANT
1860 – 1883

The End

JUST AN OL' SPOTTED HORSE

I was a young buck then; it was before I became a Ranger. I was Deputy Sheriff in Silverton, Arizona. Sheriff Ballard had brought in this no-account drifter whom he had been chasing for two weeks down below the border; he had robbed the Butterfield Stage. I don't even remember the fellow's name. I just remember the horse he was riding. She was a white mare with black spots. Nothing special about her, except she was dehydrated and half starved, with lots of rib showing. Her back was rubbed raw from the saddle that hadn't been removed from her back in God knows how long.

I don't know why I took a special liking to her, I just did. She had unusual mild blue eyes that just spoke softly to me. The Sheriff had me put her up in the livery and told me she belonged to the County now, because the drifter wasn't going to need a horse for a long while.

As I led her down the street she nosed my shoulder curiously, as if she was trying to get to know me. Her warm breath tickled my ear as she took in my scent. I just didn't understand how anyone could treat a horse that way, especially when it had such a kind, gentle nature.

When I got her to the livery, I stripped the old, weather worn saddle off her and discarded it. After that I put her in a stall. Then I gave her just a handful of grain and a good portion of grass hay. She stuck her head over the stall door and sniffed my face gently and thoroughly. I let her smell my hand and then stroked her forehead. She acted like no one had ever treated her kindly and was telling me how much she appreciated it.

"What's your name ol' girl? I know, I'll just call you, Spot." I had a white spotted dog named Spot when I was a small boy and I loved her dearly. Trouble was she got in a tangle with a rabid skunk and my Pa had to shoot her. It took me a long time to understand and forgive him for that one.

I visited Spot every chance I got for the next few weeks. I rubbed salve on her wounds and gradually added a little more grain to her diet every couple of days. Slowly her wounds healed and she began to pick up weight and fill out. I also exercised her in the corral out back of the livery one or two times every day. I guessed her to be a three or four year old.

The Sheriff called me in one morning and said he needed me to go out to George Krager's place and serve a warrant on him. The circuit judge would be coming to town that afternoon and Krager had been arrested for disturbing the peace a few weeks earlier and owed damages to a local saloon owner. It would be a routine assignment, or so I thought. Normally, the Sheriff would have me rent a mount from the livery, but this time, I asked if I could ride Spot out there since she belonged to the County anyway.

"You mean," said the Sheriff, "that white spotted mare we acquired awhile back? Well yeah, go ahead. I plum forgot about that horse."

That made me pretty dog-gone happy, I was just itching to give Spot a good ride. When I got to the Krager's homestead, after a pleasant six mile ride out, things seemed unusually quiet. It wasn't much of a place, an old adobe mud hut and a run-down wood plank barn and corral. I eased down off Spot's back and let the reins go, I knew she wouldn't wander.

I walked slowly in front of her and called out toward the adobe shack. "HEY" I said. "Anybody in there?" Then I heard a rustling noise over at the barn and looked toward the sound. Suddenly, I was pushed from behind just as a rifle shot sounded and a bullet whizzed by my ear. I stumbled forward about three steps and fell to the ground. Spot had shoved me with her nose and saved my life. Now, don't ask me how she knew that someone was about to shoot my way, she just did, that's all I know.

Peeking out from the corner of the barn door ol' George called and said, "Geet over here. That old woman's gone loco in the head."

I ducked down and hurried over to the barn. "What's goin' on here George?" I said when I got inside.

"Oh, that old woman got all crazy because I drank up all'a her home recipe." he said. I raised an eyebrow at his explanation. "We-l-l, she's the one that said it was for medicinal purposes, and I was sick. I mean, I needed a-hair-of-the-dog that bit me. You know a little nip to quite the hangover I had from last night's drinkin' with my ol' pard Norman?"

"Sure George, I understand," I said.

I called toward the house "CARLOTTA- This is Deputy Hyder," I said.

"Yeah, so?" she said from the shack.

"Listen," I said. "I don't want you to shoot me. I am the Law you know? I've come to take George in to see the Judge."

"That old coot," Carlotta said, "drank up all my medicine, and, I ain't gonna stand fer it no more, al'm a tellin' ya."

"I understand that," I said. "And, I'll make the Judge aware of it if you just let me take him in." I knew that if Carlotta had a chance to simmer down a bit she would go off the warpath and forget about shooting her husband. They did seem to care for each other though they both let the whisky bottle come between them on occasion.

"Sorry I shot at ya Deputy. My eyes ain't what they used to be. I thought you were that useless, no-count Norm Songer. Now, you got to promise me, Deputy Hyder, that you'll tell the Judge he drank up all my medicine and now the rheumatoid's got me somethin' awful."

"I promise," I said. " I'll make the Judge aware of what George has done to upset you so."

"All right then," Carlotta said, "go ahead and get him outta here."

Back in town in front of the Judge, George was fined four-dollars for disturbing the peace, because that's all he had. He was also told that he had to work weekends cleaning the saloon for the owner. This was to pay off the damages he had caused on his rampage of throwing glasses and bottles. And, after I explained the trouble between George and his wife, like I promised Carlotta I would do, the Judge gave him a night in jail for upsetting her. He didn't mind spending the night since he would have had to ride home in the dark if not for the sentence.

Later, I told the Sheriff about Spot saving my life and asked him if I could buy her from the County. "You can have that horse as far as I'm concerned," said the Sheriff. However, I insisted that I buy her for a fair price, because I didn't want any misunderstanding to come up at a future time. I wanted to know she was totally mine. The Sheriff said he felt ten-dollars was a fair price and I drew the money out of the bank and paid for her. I had the Sheriff make me a bill-of-sale so, I knew for sure I owned her without any doubt or dispute.

The next year or so was pretty peaceful around Silverton, but then there was a report of a renegade Apache raiding party in the area, and those around the town became quite anxious about it. One morning I decided to take a ride out in the desert to break the monotony of hanging around town. The Sheriff cautioned me to keep my eyes open for Indians before I left and I assured him that I would.

Spot and I had become as close as a man and an animal could over the time we had spent together. I really enjoyed riding her. She was healthy now and really liked for me to give her her head to run when we rode out in the desert.

I was out of town about two miles or so and stopped to take a drink of water and a bite out of a biscuit I had brought along. I admired the bright colors of the cactus flowers that were in bloom as I sat atop Spot sipping water out of my canteen. Then, off in the distance, a few hundred yards away I saw three riders coming hard and fast in my direction. It was three Apache warriors and they were screaming war whoops and closing on me fast. I corked my canteen in a hurry and swung Spot around to head back toward town hell-bent-for-leather.

Those undernourished Indian ponies were no match for the now recuperated horse I had nursed back to health. Spot gained a full lead on the warriors in short order.

When we were within sight of town, about three-quarters of a mile away with a good lead we suddenly came upon a dry wash at full stride. Spot stretched and leaped in the air right into the wash and landed full force in the fork of a wild oak tree growing up out of the edge of the wash.

I was thrown headlong into the center of the wash and to my good fortune landed on a soft sandbar. Spot wasn't so fortunate; she was stuck tightly in the fork of the tree with all four legs up off the ground about three feet. She struggled desperately to free herself to no avail. I regained my senses realizing I wasn't hurt much more than having the wind knocked out of me. I then stumbled to my feet and trudged across the soft sand to her. I could see she was in distress and was starting to have problems breathing. I grabbed the rains and tried to calm her, stroking her nose. That seemed to settle her some.

"Easy girl," I said in as gentle and reassuring voice as I could. "We're going to get you out of there," I said, though I had no idea how I could accomplish that task with a twelve hundred pound horse.

Tears welled up in my eyes, though I tried to shake it off. I looked into her soft blue eyes which were wild with anxiety and I knew that what I had just promised was going to be next to impossible to accomplish before she stifled or died of distress.

I climbed to the top of the wash to see where my pursuers were and saw that they were riding away. They probably gave up the chase because we were so close to town, also I wanted to see what the situation was from the other side of where Spot was hung up. It didn't look any better from behind. She was fighting and kicking with her back legs and I knew that if I was going to do her any good at all I needed to calm her down. Already her rear haunches were rubbed raw and red from the struggling. She was wedged right behind her rib cage and in front of her thighs. Her front feet now just did touch the ground, but this didn't help any, because it put a lot of pressure and weight on her lungs which was causing her breathing to be distressed.

I tried desperately to think of what to do. How was I going to lift a twelve hundred pound horse up out of there? I thought about running to town for help, but I didn't want to leave her, besides there was no way she would last that long. I had to do something now, but what?

I went back around front and got hold of the reins again. She struggled and jerked trying to free herself; it was no use, her strength was slipping away fast. Once again I calmed her by speaking softly, trying hard to hold back my own emotions because of the futility of the situation. I had never felt so helpless; what a freak of a thing to happen. What in the world could I do? My mind ran wild with stupid ideas that wouldn't work; block and tackle, a leverage bar, I just couldn't think straight. There just was no time to get any kind of help. I was so confused, I lost track of time, so I'm not sure how much time had passed, somewhere around an hour was my best guess.

Spot's struggling lessened considerably and her eyes where losing their personality. Her lips and tongue were darkened blue, almost black. I knew what I had to do now; I didn't want her to suffocate, that was no way for her to die. I rubbed her forehead gently and kissed her nose. Then, I turned and took two steps away from her as I pulled my Remington .44 out of the holster and thumbed back the hammer.

"DANG IT. Why did this have to happen?" I said out loud. I heard her breathing behind me, it was forced and shallow, she was slipping away and there was nothing else to do but relieve her suffering. "DAMN." I turned and fired. It was over; Spot was gone. A warm tear forced its way out and rolled slowly down my cheek.

I walked into town, got an ax and a shovel and then walked back out to where she was. I cut a limb off one side of the fork and that freed her from its deadly grasp. I dug a grave at the bottom of the decline of the wash and rolled and leveraged her into it. It was quite difficult and draining, but I was determined to see to it she was buried proper. Then I took that ax and cut that tree off at the ground and dug down and cut as much of the roots out as I possibly could.

I have never forgotten Spot, she is still the best horse I have ever ridden, and I have rode many over my years as a Ranger. I can still picture her soft blue, gentle eyes, and that has been more than thirty years ago.

THE END

Dedicated to Betty and the memory of 'Boo', a spotted horse who died tragically.

PAL

"NO- NO. This wasn't the way it was supposed to turn out," said Pal as his brain burned and the image of his kid brother Bobby haunted his mind. Lying there in the dusty street, face down, a weak hand reaching out for help. Pal was too scared and concerned about his own skin to turn and go back for him. "Besides," Pal had said to himself and rationalized, "Bobby was dying anyway. Nobody, could have lived through that hail of .44 and .45 slugs."

Pal wasn't his real name. It was what his younger brother had called him ever since they were little and Bobby was old enough to talk. Nick always called Bobby his little pal, especially when he wanted to con him into or out of something. So, Bobby started calling Nick, Pal early on and the name had stuck; even his friends, who were few, called him that.

Pal had always taken advantage of the fact that his little brother was slow of mind. It didn't bother Pal in the least using him as a scapegoat to keep himself out of trouble neither. Bobby never got upset with him, in fact, he worshipped his older brother and Pal could talk him into about anything. Now, because Pal had persuaded him into helping him rob the Black Ridge City Bank, Bobby lay in the street mortally wounded. A dozen cowboys had come out of the saloon across the street from the bank and opened fire on them as they made their retreat out of town.

Pal's muscles quaked and shivered in stiff hot pain as the last sight of his brother burned in his brain again. He selfishly wiped it out of his conscience and looked down at his swollen arm. His fingers on his right hand were so puffy that he couldn't move them. The waves of severe pain in his hip caused him to wince and whimper like a hurt, starving little pup.

"How could it end like this?" he wondered. "He had planned it so carefully." For the last two years of his thirty-month sentence he had planned out how he would get even with the town of Black Ridge, Texas. "Rob the bank," he had reasoned. "That would get them where it hurts and give him money enough to enjoy life down in Old Mexico for a long while. They would pay for his two and a half years of hard labor in that hot, dirty, stinking hole of a prison camp."

Because of his youthful age of eighteen, Pal was not hanged for cattle rustling like his two older partners. Instead, the judge had said, "I will be lenient with you and sentence you to thirty months of hard labor." He added and said, "This will mellow you young man, and mature you, so you can be a productive citizen in the community."

"BULL," Pal had lashed out in anger and threatened, "I'll get even with y'all somehow." So, he had painstakingly planned the bank robbery. The thing was, he had no way of knowing about the saloon full of trail drovers waiting for their ramrod to come to town. Someone had yelled, "BANK ROBBERY", and they had all piled out of the saloon to see what was going on.

Bobby missed the stirrup hurriedly trying to mount his horse and it ran off leaving him standing in the street. He never even pulled his pistol, he just ran on foot down the street after his brother as he rode hell-bent toward the edge of town. With bullets buzzing by his ears Pal's heart pounded in mortal fear. The drovers unloaded hot lead on the one target they knew they could hit and Bobby fell in the street face down as Pal glanced back over his shoulder. Overtaken with fear he shut his eyes, turned his head and just kept on riding hard and fast.

Pal had planned everything so carefully, or so he thought. Two fresh horses stood ready just over the next ridge. Knowing what a good tracker the old Texas Ranger Sheriff Sy Wood was, Pal had weighted sandbags ready to put on the horses they had ridden out of town. He figured this more than likely would lead the posse off track. They would cover the trail of their fresh mounts until they got to the river and then ride down stream for a mile or so while the posse chased after the weighted horses thinking it was the two of them. Pal had learned this trick from a notorious Mexican bandit he was in prison with.

The saloon full of cattle drovers and the rattlesnake in the middle of the trail were things Pal certainly had not counted on. As he guided his horse through a narrow rock pass his horse spooked by the rattlesnake reared high and dumped him on his backside. It was a small snake but, it had latched on to the meaty part of his forearm and pumped a potent amount of venom in. The horse ran off and

Pal was not only snake bit, but had apparently shattered his hip in the fall. He had painfully dragged himself out of the heat of the day to the shade of a rocky crag. There he now sat in an unnatural position because of his pain, leaning against a huge boulder.

Pal's flesh felt like it was on fire and all the muscles in his body screamed in agony. His muscles hurt so much that the pain in his hip was reduced to a dull numbness. His stomach tightened into a knot and his throat filled with sickening fluid that choked him and demanded to be expelled. He gagged and vomited violently. "O-oh," he moaned and said, "What I wouldn't give for a cool drink of water."

While waiting on the next wave of pain and violent sickness he pictured in his mind sitting in the nearby shallow river with cool water running over his body. "It was only a half mile or so away. If only I could get there somehow?" Looking down at his arm again and feeling the weakness surge throughout his body he knew that was an impossibility. He came to the realization that he was going to die there where he sat under the shade of the rocky crag.

Pal reached painfully across to his right hip, pulled out his Starr revolver with his left hand, and adjusted it. When he got it across to his left side his hand dropped to the dirt in mere exhaustion. The strength to raise the pistol to his head was not there. He really didn't have the courage to end his life with his pistol anyway, so he sat frozen in time, his mind blank for the longest time.

No matter how much he tried to dismiss the thought of his younger brother lying in the street, reaching out, it still returned to his mind and agonized him. Then a vision appeared, his mother lying on her deathbed, weak and frail. He relived her death as if it was happening again, right there and then. She weakly said, "Nick, it's up to you now. Take care of Bobby. He gets along quite well by himself, but he still needs someone to look after him. Your father, drinking the way he does, he can't look after anyone. So, you must promise me, you will take good care of him."

"Ma, please don't die. You don't have to go," said Pal tearfully.

"Don't worry son. I will be in a better place. Now, promise me, you will look after your brother so I can rest in peace."

"All right, I will Ma," said Pal Then he begged again. "But Ma, please, don't die."

His mother reached out and caressed his cheek, "Don't worry son it will be all right. Now, get your brother in here, so I can say good-bye."

Before Pal returned to her with Bobby she had passed away. Their father lay drunk in a saloon that day and Pal never spoke to him again after that. It was the worst day in Pal's life, he felt bitter and refused to attend the funeral. He thought his mother, wanting to escape her lonely miserable existence, had somehow left him on purpose, though he knew that tuberculosis had been what killed her.

He was fifteen at the time and went from bad to worse, constantly in trouble after that. Pal completely dismissed looking after his brother as his mother had asked. He had not even given her instructions a thought since that time until now. For the first time in Pal's life he felt regret for his past conduct. There was no way he could make it right now. His brother had paid the price for trusting in him. Pal realized he was no better than his father was by not taking care of his responsibility to look after his brother. If only he had not persuaded Bobby with his smooth talk, Bobby would not have ended up in the street shot down like a mad dog.

Suddenly, Pal realized that a voice was calling his name. It sounded hollow to him, as if it were coming from the inside of a cave. He felt a blessed coolness on his parched dry lips. Someone was lifting his head and giving him water. "Ma," he said.

"No, young man I'm not your ma," a voice said. It was Sheriff Wood.

Pal opened his eyes and stared into the man's face. He had always thought of Sy Wood as a hard, unforgiving man, but now he saw compassion in Sheriff Wood's face.

"Al'm gonna die, ain't I Sheriff?" said Pal. The Sheriff only answered with his expression and somber eyes. "Don't feel bad Sheriff, I deserve it. I caused my brother to die in the street and didn't even have the guts to go back and help him. I was too worried about my own skin."

"Your brother's not dead, son," Sheriff Wood said. "Oh, it will take him a while to heal but, he ain't gonna die. Least that's what the Doc said after he took those three slugs out of his back."

Pal pleaded as meaningful as his weakened state would allow him and said, "Al'm ter'ible sorry for what I done. The money Sheriff, it's on my horse. He ran off after he throwed me. If'n you get the money back, can't ya let Bobby go? He ain't no bad man. He just done it because I goaded him into it. He ain't too awful bright and he'll do most anything I ask him to do. It's my fault, I mean if'n you get the money back and all?"

"We already found your horse and recovered the money," said the Sheriff. "And yeah, I s'pose I could talk to the new Circuit Judge, he is an old friend of mine, and have him go easy on your brother, since we got the money back and nobody was hurt except him. I know how your brother is and he's got a good heart. Sure son I can do that just this once for the sake of a remorseful dyin' man."

Pal felt numb all over, the pain was gone and he felt as if he was drifting on the water. A slit of a smile formed on one side of his face. The vision of his mother in her bed appeared to him again. This time she had a wide smile and bright glad eyes that told Pal that he had done what she had asked him to do. Then the vision started to fade into gray and then total darkness fell on Pal and he was gone.

THE END

THE RANSOM

On a ledge overlooking the H&H Railroad line that ran up the side of the Ve·loz River Pass, Dale sat on his heels, crouched down behind a large boulder waiting. Right on time the powerful steam locomotive started to make the long pull up the mountainside. Black smoke bellowed a long trail and great clouds of steam puffed out the sides of the iron horse. It struggled and slowed to a crawl pulling the long steep grade.

Dale's light blue eyes watched the steam enginc pass before him with such intense anticipation that there wasn't anything else on earth happening at that moment. Dale timed his jump accurately and carefully, because one miscalculation would mean sudden death on the jagged rocks far below. When the trains coal-tender was in just the right position, Dale's eyes widened and he made his leap. Landing hard and solid on the back of the coal pile he struggled to catch his balance. Then he started working his way atop the coal toward the engine.

Meanwhile at the top of the hill, Sam and Cal Newberry sat on their horses waiting patiently to execute their part of the plan. The train slowly moved into the picture, then jerked to a sudden halt. The engine, a coal-tender, a long brightly painted coach car, a boxcar and the caboose were all that made up the train.

Sam and Cal jumped off their horses and ran to the steps of the private car. The long red coach had a large gold colored wagon wheel with H&H in the

Center painted on its side. This was the H&H Railroad companies logo.

Cal found the door locked so, with all his force behind it, he smashed into the door of the car with his shoulder. The door gave way with less effort than Cal had expected and he tumbled in across the floor, pistol still in hand. A man in a pin striped suit sitting behind a desk jumped to his feet and pulled a long barreled pistol from a shoulder holster and fired at Cal. Cal shrieked in pain, dropped his pistol and grabbed for his leg.

Sam, who was inside the car now, stepped toward the man behind the desk with a Smith & Wesson Schofield revolver raised, cocked and pointed at the man's face. The man stood firm, pistol aimed at Cal.

"I don't wanna kill you mister," Sam said. "But, you ain't gonna shoot my brother again without dyin' for it."

Keeping his pistol trained on Cal the man looked over at Sam. Sam saw no hint of fear in the man's cool gray eyes. Steadying his aim Sam said, "I mean it mister. Put it down or I'll take your head off."

The man with the long barreled pistol behind the desk looked over to another man in a suit sitting at a table by the window. Across from this man sat a stately black haired woman with flashing dark blue eyes, wearing an elegant red and black dress. She had a lace hanky to her lips.

"Better put it down, Jim," said the man at the table. The young fella means business."

"Are you sure, Brad?" he said. "I think I can take him out. Maybe put away the one on the floor."

"Not this time, Jim," the man at the table said. "I am curious to see what this is about."

"All right Brad. You're the boss," Jim said. Then he reluctantly put the pistol down on the desk and slid it toward Sam.

"Thanks mister," Sam said to the man at the table. "I didn't wanna kill him."

"Make no mistake about it, youngster," the man replied. "Jim would have killed you and your brother if I had told him to."

"I take it you're Bradley Hinckley?" said Sam. "That's right," said the man at table, "What's this all about?"

Before Sam had a chance to answer, Dale herded the engineer, the fireman, the tinder boy and the conductor through the door.

Sam rushed to his brother who was on the floor holding his wounded leg. Cal's pant leg was soaked with blood and his eyes were glazed, obviously he was concerned about how bad he might be hurt.

The blue eyed lady came over. "I was a nurse during the war," she said softly. "I can help, if you will allow me."

The woman's soft caring blue eyes reminded Sam of his mother. "Sure. Thanks," said Sam as he stepped back to watch. There was a lot of blood and Sam was worried about his brother.

"The bullet passed through his thigh," the woman said. "He will heal if I can stop the bleeding. Are there any medical supplies on the train?" she said.

"Some in the caboose," said the conductor.

Hinckley came over to join the group, the woman looked up at him expectantly. "I'm going to need those bandages to stop this bleeding, Brad," she said.

"You had better go and get them supplies, youngster," Hinckley said to Sam. "I'll pour some hot water from the teakettle if you need it." The lady answered Brad with a nod.

Sam's thoughts went back to two days previous and he wondered how he had ever let himself be talked into this scheme in the first place. He had been setting up the last few letters of the front page of the Daily Sentinel when his brother Cal had come into the newspaper office.

"Come on outside," Cal had said excitedly. "I found a way to get even with the H&H Railroad."

"What now, Cal? I got work to do," said Sam. "When did you get back in town anyway?"

"About two hours ago. I've been loadin' cattle down at the stock yards," said Cal as he slapped dust out of his hat on the leg of his chaps. "Now, come outside. I want you to meet this fella."

"DOG-GONE IT, Cal" said Sam. "You otta know better than stir up all that dust in here."

"Oh... sorry," said Cal, "Come on Sam."

"I can't be foolin' around with you or your hare brained schemes today, Cal," Sam said. "I'll lose my job if I don't get this done on time. Mr. Thomas said he has had enough of my leavin' work with you and me not meetin' his deadlines because of it. He said the only reason he ain't fired me before now is because I do such a good job on setting things up."

"Well, al'm your brother. And, by gosh I take priority over everyone else, job or what," Cal said. "Besides, I got somebody I want you to meet. I ain't askin' you to go no-wheres, 'cept outside here for two lousy minutes. That ain't so much to ask now, is it?"

"Two minutes, Cal," said Sam. "That's all you get. Two minutes."

"That's all I'm askin'. Now come on," said Cal. Sam pulled off his apron and looked through the front window at the stranger standing outside. A tall lanky stranger was looking around nervously with his head down. It was obvious that he was keeping under the shadow of his hat to hide his face. Sam figured the fellow to be around Cal's age, who was eighteen, and he looked to be covered in trail dust like Cal.

Sam stepped outside with his older brother who introduced the stranger right off. "This here's Dale Tremble. Dale, this here's my kid brother, Sam. He'll be a goin' with us on this deal," Cal said.

"*Kid*...shore enough," said Dale. "We can't be baby watchin' on this job Cal."

"I ain't no baby by a long way," said Sam. "I'm almost seventeen. And, I can thrash the daylights out of a stick like you any day of the week."

"Ya talk big for a little feller," said Dale as he grinned.

Sam started for Dale with his fist doubled up and fire in his dark blue eyes. Cal caught Sam's arm and snatched him back right before he took a poke at Dale.

"Come on Sam calm down here," said Cal.

"Dale and me's got a plan. It'll get our money from the H&H and then some besides. You wanna make 'em pay fer what they done, don't ya?"

"You know I do," Sam said.

"Well, listen up then," Cal said. "Dale and me's been figgerin' this deal for the past three days. You see, Dale was in the telegraph office in Johnston three days ago to pick up a message for the trail boss. This telegram comes in while he's there sayin' Bradley W. Hinckley will be comin' in on the seventeenth."

"So what?" Sam said impatiently. "I mean, what's that gotta do with us getting' any money from the H&H Rail Road?"

"Yer dumber'n a box of rocks," said Dale and laughed sarcastically. Cal had to catch and hold Sam back a second time.

"Come on now you two," Cal said. "We gotta get along and cooperate or we ain't gonna be able to pull this deal off."

"All right, Cal," Sam said reluctantly. "But, you tell this ya-hoo to watch his yap or I'll close it for 'em."

"Watch the cracks, all right Dale? We need to talk serious about this deal fella's," said Cal. "Not be fussin' 'mongst ourselves." Cal gave Sam a hard look.

"Yeah, yeah. What's the plan," Sam said.

"You see," Cal said, "Dale's told me that ol' Hinckley's got his own private railroad car. An', it'll be comin' up the Ve·loz River Pass on its way to Johnston. When that train pulls the long grade up the pass, it'll be at a crawl by the time it gets to the top. What we'll do is, jump the train and stop it at the top of the pass. Then, we'll hold ol' Hinckley for ransom."

"Right Cal," Sam said sarcastically. "Come on now. Don't you think, ol' Hinckley will have forty dozen railroad agents on board to protect him. Heck, man," Sam said as he shook his head. "I got to go back to work. I ain't got time for this stuff today."

"Wait a minute now Sam. Dog-gone-it listen and hear me out," said Cal. "We got this figgered al'm a tellin' you."

"Forget this little kid, Cal" said Dale. "We don't need 'em. We can pull this off our own-selves."

"No, you wait," said Cal. "My brother goes or I don't."

"Please Sam, listen to the whole thing," Cal said pleading with his brother. "I need your help on this. Look, Dale knows that Hinckley doesn't have any guards on board. Hinckley thinks he can take care of himself, so he doesn't have anybody with him for protection, 'ceptin' the train crew and his bookkeeper."

"And, what makes ol' Dale here such an expert on Hinckley?" said Sam.

"He worked for the H&H Rail Road for almost a year and he knows," said Cal.

"All right. Who's gonna pay the ransom money?" said Sam sarcastically. "And, just how are we gonna get away after we stop this train at the top of the pass? That's one treacherous hill to ride down on horseback."

"I told you. We got everything figgered," Cal said. "When Haze, Hinckley's partner comes with the ransom money we'll just simply unhook the car from the rest of the train and ride it the six miles back down the mountain. It'll take men on horseback two hours or better to ride down that narrow rim. Coastin' in the railroad car we'll be down that grade in less than twenty minutes. There's no sharp curves to worry about on the way down and we'll have plenty of time to get away on the fresh mounts we'll have a waitin'."

"You know..." Sam said as he lifted his visor and scratched his head, "It might just work at that. You're sure about there bein' no head-busters on that train?"

"Dog-gone right al'm shore," said Dale. "I was tinder boy on that train for eight stinkin' months."

"What about my job here?" said Sam.

"What about it?" said Cal. "I mean, who needs a job with all the money we'll have after this."

"How much you planin' on askin' for anyways?" said Sam.

Dale said interrupting, "Fifteen thousand."
"FIFTEEN thousand," said Sam. "Ain't that a bit much?"

"They can afford it," said Cal. "Besides, they killed our pa and caused ma so much grief that she died before her time."

"I suppose that's true enough," Sam said. "Wait'a minute here. How we gonna deliver a ransom note to Haze when we're at the train up at the pass?"

"Haven't I told you we got it all covered," said Cal. "We got this kid who's gonna deliver a note to Haze a little before we stop the train. It's all a matter of timin'. Haze is just north of here with a road crew. Sam, I tell you it's all set if you're with us."

"Shouldn't we maybe, have guns?" said Sam. Cautiously Cal looked to his left and right to see if anyone was watching. When he saw it was clear he pulled back his jacket to reveal a large caliber pistol stuck in his belt.

Dale looked around too, then he slipped a .44 Schofield revolver to Sam. "You think you can handle that son?" he said.

"Don't you worry about me," said Sam as he stuffed the pistol in the front of his pants and pulled his shirt out over it. "I've handled guns before."

"Good," said Dale with a smile. "It's all set then. Two days from now, the seventeenth we'll meet behind the livery stables. And, we'll be on our way to five thousand dollars apiece... Hot-Damn."

"Al'ma goin' down an' get me a drink to warsh the trail dust out'a my gullet," said Cal. "See you later, Sam."

"Yeah. I got to get back to work," Sam said.

Cal and Dale headed for the nearest saloon. Sam went back into the newspaper office.

Now, there they were, Cal laying on the floor wounded and bleeding and Sam wondering what to do next.

"Come on you," Sam said to the conductor. "Show me where these medical supplies are. Dale, you settle everybody down. I'll be right back with those bandages. Cal, you just hang on there. You'll be all right."

"Hur-ry," said Dale as he moaned.

"Let's get this fellow over to the couch," said Hinckley as he instructed the engineer and the others.

Sam and the conductor were back with the medical supplies in short order. The woman went right to work cleaning and bandaging Cal's leg while he lay on a large couch. Dale was sitting on the desk, Hinckley and the man that shot Cal were sitting at the table and the rest were sitting against the wall in chairs.

With a wrinkled brow and narrowed dark accusing eyes the conductor said to Dale, "I know you... I fired you butt for pilfering here while back."

Dale slid off the desk and walked over to the conductor. His light blue eyes blazed with anger as he switched his pistol to his left hand and slapped the conductor across the face with his right hand. The conductor nearly fell out of his chair. He straightened himself and gave Dale a hateful burning glare. A stream of blood ran out of the conductor's nose coloring his heavy gray mustache.

"I'll shoot you dead if you open yer mouth again," said Dale.

"That's enough Dale," said Sam. "Let's just take care of business here and not cause no more trouble than necessary. We got enough to worry about with Cal bein' shot an' all."

"Yeah. Well this fella I otta shoot anyway. Just for the principle of the thing," said Dale.

"Just what is this about?" said Hinckley. "I mean, if you want to rob us there is about two-hundred dollars in the safe over there behind the desk. You are welcome to it. I'm sorry but I don't carry large amounts of cash with me for obvious reasons."

Cal winced as he sat up. "Check it out Dale," he said.

Dale went to the safe which was open slightly. He pulled the door back and took out the cash. "He's tellin' the truth," said Dale. "Ain't no cash in here, 'cept'n a couple hundred. And there's this here tin can...can of soup, vegetable-beef. Imagine that will ya. Vegetable-beef soup in a dab-burn can."

Sam looked at Hinckley curiously. "It's an investment I have been considering," said Hinckley. "Sorry boys, that's all there is."

Dale stuffed the money in his coat pocket. Admiring it, he tossed the can up in the air and caught it.

"You know, I'm not surprised at your friend there," Hinckley said as he nodded toward Dale. "But, you and your brother just don't seem comfortable with this robbery business. And, I am a pretty good judge of character."

Sam pulled back a curtain and stared out a window. "It ain't something we do every day if that's what you mean," he said from behind the curtain.

"No," said Cal who sat close by. "But takin' money from you ain't what we'd call stealin' anyways. It's getting' even. It's getting' back what rightfully belongs to us is the way I see it."

"Whatever do you mean?" Hinckley said.

"I'll tell you what he means," Sam said. "Your man Race Tuttle killed our pa and then took advantage of our ma when the H&H bought our farm for a lousy two dollars an acre. Our farm would be worth ten times that much now. Our ma was so grieved over loosin' pa and our farm that she just gave up and died not long after."

"Tuttle, h-uh? Well, Race Tuttle was Haze's man," said Hinckley. "He took care of buying land for the railroad until he was shot over a card game three months ago. Just, how do you boy's plan on getting even? I don't see any way you can get your farm back."

"It ain't the farm we want now," said Cal. "It's long gone. We want the money we were cheated out of, that's what we want."

"You've already seen that I don't have any cash here," said Hinckley.

"Your partner Haze is bringin' the money," said Sam who was still peering out the window. "He should be here in just a little while."

"You are trying to hold me for ransom?" said Hinckley with a laugh. "Can you believe that, Jim? They're asking Haze to pay a ransom for my life."

Jim gave half a smile and said, "You should have let me shoot 'em, Brad. Now, you don't stand much of a chance."

"I don't think a man in your position should have anything to laugh about," Sam said.

"Well, I'll tell you youngster," said Hinckley. "If you're waiting for Carlton F. Haze to pay any ransom money for me, you had just better not hold your breath."

Dale came over to the table. He leaned on his knuckles and looked down at Hinckley from across the table. "And, why's that?" he asked. "He's your partner ain't he?"

"Sure he is," Jim said. "But he don't like it much. It would suit him just fine to see Brad out of the way."

"He would shoot me himself if he thought he could get away with it," Hinckley said. "Then he could have the whole company to himself and run it the way he wants to."

Cal looked at Sam. "What're we gonna do now Sam?", he said.

"I don't know Cal. I gotta think," said Sam.

"You don't believe that wild ass tale, do ya?" said Dale.

"I don't know," said Sam sharply.

"Believe me boys," said Hinckley. "It would please Carlton Haze to no end if I was out of the picture. Jim and me are the only things keeping him in check. Jim is my bodyguard and accountant and he is good at his job. If it weren't for his watching over the company's books, why we would end up in bankruptcy in no time.

"Why don't you boys tell me about what happened with your parents and the farm."

"Ain't a whole lot to tell," said Cal. "Race Tuttle and two other fella's came out to the farm and tried to get our pa to sell. He told them he had no mind to sell the farm and that the four dollars an acre they were offerin' wasn't enough if he was. Tuttle told him that he would change his mind or suffer the consequences. Then Pa said he wasn't about to change his mind and that he wouldn't be threatened by him or the H&H Railroad. He told them to get out of his house before he threw them out. Tuttle said he had two days to change his mind then they left.

"Two days later after dark, we had been in bed for about an hour when Pa woke us up to a house full of smoke. We all ran outside and was throwin' buckets of water on the house when the barn broke out in flames. It was useless. We couldn't get either one of the fires under control. Pa ran around the side of the barn to let our horses out of the corral. We heard a shot. When we went around to the side we found him dead, he'd been shot in the back. Two men were riding off in the distance.

"A week or so after my pa's funeral, Tuttle and the other two came out to the farm and told my ma she had better sell because, there was no way she could rebuild the place. Tuttle said he was doin' her a favor by offerin' two dollars an acre. She didn't know what to do so she accepted his measly offer. About eight months later she died a broken woman.

"That's it. That's the story. And, your railroad was responsible whether you were directly involve or not."

"I am sorry about your parents boys," Hinckley said. "But, let me tell you a little bit about the way progress works."

Hinckley got up and paced the floor as he talked. "You see my parents and grandparents and probably yours too, trudged out to this country in big wagons with large wheels on them. That's why I chose a large wagon wheel as a logo for the H&H Railroad. These people came out west and fought the Indians and took away their land, to settle it, to build on it, to civilize it. To do that they had to kill the Indian and those they didn't kill they stuck on reservations. I am not saying it was right, mind you. But, that's the way progress works sometimes.

"Then the war started between the states and we killed many on both sides. Men took land and control. It had to be done in order for progress to be made. I know youngsters because, I fought in that war. I was in the Navy of the losing side, Jim and I served together. That was my ship there, she was a tall ship," Hinckley said proudly as he pointed to a painting of a ship hanging on the wall. Under the picture hung an ivory handled, nickel-plated .36 caliber pistol.

"She was sunk, a very great loss indeed. My ship wasn't all I lost due to the war either. But, I recovered, made some wise investments after the war. That's how I got involved with Carlton Haze and met Miss Priscilla Kates there who has been my dear friend and constant companion ever since."

Everyone looked over at the woman on the couch sitting with Cal. She smiled and nodded lady like.

"You see," said Hinckley as he continued. "I know progress can be unfair, and deadly at times. Of course, that is no excuse for what my unscrupulous partner allowed to happen to you and your family. But, if he hadn't done it, someone else probably would have. Now, I can't bring back your mother and father but, I can see to it that you get a fair price for that farm you lost. You say it was worth ten times the two dollars an acre they gave your mother? How many acres did you have?"

"There was two hundred and thirty acres," said Sam from the window.

"All right, Jim," Hinckley said. "If I have it figured right that would be two times, ten times two hundred and thirty acres. What does that come to?"

After a short pause to figure in his head, Jim said, "Four thousand six hundred dollars."

"Draw up a bank draft in these two boy's name for that amount," Hinckley said.

"You are joking aren't you Brad?" Jim said.
"No, Jim," said Hinckley. "You know I don't joke around when it comes to money."

"That's minus the four hundred sixty dollars they already got. Right?"

"No Jim," said Hinckley. "The whole amount. Four thousand six hundred dollars. These boy's lost their parents over this deal."

"All right, Brad. You're the boss and if you're gonna let these boys get away with that I guess I have nothing to say about it," Jim said. He went over to the desk and took out a bank draft and dunked a quill pen in the inkwell. He paused, "You are sure about this, Brad?"

"Yes Jim, fill it out. I do appreciate you looking out for my best interest as usual though," Hinckley said. Jim started writing.

"We don't need your charity mister," Cal said.

"You would rather rob me and try to justify it because your mother was cheated. That doesn't make you any better than my partner, Haze. Besides, it isn't charity. You said yourself the farm was worth ten times what your mother was paid for it. I would like to have the privilege of at least righting that part of the wrong that my unscrupulous partner did.

"I'll tell you youngster, if Haze shows up it won't be money he will have with him. It will be the sheriff and fifty or sixty armed railroad men."

"Com'on you fellas," said Dale. "Don't fall for that line of bull. He's tryin' to get us out of here before Haze gets here with the fifteen thousand. Why settle for under five thousand when we can have fifteen."

"What do you say, Conductor?" asked Sam. "Is Mr. Hinckley tellin' the truth about Haze?"

"I wouldn't trust Haze no farther than I can throw this train. But, I'll tell you I've never known Mr. Hinckley to lie or be unfair about anything. As far as that fella there is concerned," the Conductor said nodding toward Dale. "I would steer shy of him. He's headed for the hangman's noose."

Dale raised his pistol, aimed it at the conductor face and cocked it, then he said, "I'll burn you down you mouthy son-of-a..."

"DALE," Sam said. "Stop it. You put it down or you'll have to deal with me."

"I ain't afraid of you," said Dale. "Yer jest a little snotty noised kid."

"He ain't no kid," said Cal. "Now, rest that ir'n or I'll deal with you myself."

Dale paused thinking for a moment, then lowered the pistol down to his side and reset the hammer. "Count yerself lucky today Conductor," he said. Sam again peering out the window from behind the curtain said, "Well, Mr. Hinckley was right about one thing. Here comes Haze. And, he's got the High Sheriff and about twenty or thirty armed men with him."

"That's just dandy," said Cal. "I said in the note for him not, to bring anybody. 'specially not the law."

"You jess tell 'em out there we'll kill his partner if they don't leave the money and clear out," said Dale.

"Don't you listen to nothin," said Sam. "Haze ain't gonna pay no ransom money."

"Yer not really gonna fall for this are ya?" questioned Dale.

"Yeah. I believe it," said Sam.

"Cal," Dale said, "talk some sense into that brother of yers. We're gonna end up leavin' outta here with nothin' if ya don't."

"I think you're the one who ain't makin' any sense. Hinckley said Haze would come with a pack of armed men, and he has. What we gotta figger out now is how to get outta here without getting' all shot up."

"I ain't goin' nowheres till I got that fifteen thousand in my hand. Or, before I put a bullet in yer lyin' skull there Hinckley," Dale said shaking his pistol at Hinckley.

"I told you to put it away, Dale," Cal said.

"I ain't. I've had enough of you and yer kid brother. I didn't plan this out to have it go sour on me now."

"HEY. You's inside that coach," a voice called from outside. "This here's Sheriff Hardgrove speakin' ta ya. I got a heavily armed posse out here. You's all had just better come on out with your hands held high. There ain't no way for you's to get away."

Dale went over to one of the windows and broke the glass out with his pistol barrel. He shouted out and said, "We'll kill these folks in here if ya don't deliver the money and clear on out."

"I'm Carlton Haze," said a voice from the posse. "I want to let you know that I won't give in to a bunch of hooligan's demands. You had just better do what the Sheriff says or we will blast you out of there."

"And, it'll be in short order if you's don't come on out real quick with those hands held high," said the Sheriff.

"I mean what al'm sayin' too," said Dale. "I'll start shootin' folks if ya don't back off and leave that fifteen thousand."

"We are not going to cooperate with criminals I told you," said Haze. "You have ten minutes to make up your mind before we blast you out of there."

Dale turned away from the window and slid down the wall to a sitting position on the floor. He rested his pistol on his leg and hung his head between knees. "How we gonna get out of this?" Dale said. "They're gonna shoot their way in here in just a few minutes. Hinckley's right that's one stubborn son-of-a-gun out there. He don't care if he kills every one of us."

Hinckley looked at Cal and said, "Just how were you boys planning on getting away anyhow?"

"We stopped the train while it was still on the grade on purpose," said Cal. "Dale's already uncoupled the car from the rest of the train; all we have to do is release the brake and we'll be coastin' back down the hill and be at the bottom long before anyone can make it down on horseback.

"Did you really mean what you said about givin' us the money for our farm?" Cal said.

"Sure I did," said Hinckley. "All you have to do is tell Jim who you want that draft made out to."

"You're not gonna send a posse after us after we let you go?" Cal said.

"No. I won't do that. You have my word," said Hinckley.

"What about Haze?" said Cal. "Ain't he gonna think you paid us the ransom money yerself?"

"That draft is on my private expense account," said Hinckley. "He won't question it because, he won't know anything about it."

Sam, who had been listening with interest said, "Fair enough Mr. Hinckley. You're a fair man. And, not only that I think it's the only chance we got to get out of this deal with our skins and the money we're entitled to."

"All right there, Jim," said Sam. "You make that draft out to Calvin and Samuel Newberry."

"Dale," said Sam as he pointed to the other side of the coach with the Schofield. "You crawl on out one of those windows over there and release that break. I'll keep you covered in case someone outside sees you and wants to take a shot at you."

"Wait jest a dog-gone minute here. What about me?" said Dale. "I don't get nothin' outta this?"

"Me and Cal will make it right with you, Dale," Sam said. "You otta know us better than that. Now, hurry up before they start shootin' out there."

Dale pulled a chair over to a window on the opposite side of the coach. He threw open the sash stepped up on the chair, slid through and dropped to the ground between the hillside and the coach. Dale ran up and released the brake on the front of the coach. Slowly at first the coach and the caboose started to slip away from the engine, coal-car and the boxcar. Dale jumped on the landing of the coach and ducked inside through the door. As he did someone from the posse fired a shot that splintered the wood doorframe beside Dale's head. The splintering wood stung Dale's face. "OUCH" he said loudly. Dale's face was cut and bloodied on one side.

"You okay, Dale?" said Sam.

"It stings some, but I'll be all right." Dale said as he patted the side of his face with his bandanna.

The coach and the caboose picked up speed quickly as they coasted down the narrow rim. The posse tried to follow, but the rim was too treacherous and the coach was traveling to fast for them to keep up as was planned.

The coach and the caboose sped along rapidly down the long grade. The coach traveled much faster than anyone had really anticipated, yet since it was a relatively straight run down the six-mile slope the cars held the track well. When the track leveled out into the valley below the cars began to slow down.

Sam stepped out on the coach landing to look. "We're about there, Dale," he said. "Better get on that brake."

"Right," said Dale and he went out and started twisting down the brake wheel. The car wheels made a horrible deafening screeching sound as the railroad cars slowed and finally came to a complete halt. Dale and Sam came back inside the coach.

"Let's help Cal out to the horses," said Sam, "and we'll be on our way."

"Nope, we won't," Dale said.

"What do you mean, no?" questioned Sam.

Dale pointed his pistol at Jim who was still sitting behind the desk and said, "I mean if ol' Jim there can write you all a draft for forty-five hundred, he can write me one for another ten thousand. Now, get to writin' Jim ol' pal."

"We ain't gonna do this," said Cal.

"That's right," agreed Sam.

"You fella's made yer deal an' now al'm makin' mine," said Dale. Dale looked back at Jim who hadn't made a move. Pointing the pistol at Jim he said, "I told you to get to writin'"

With a stone cold stare Jim said, "I don't believe I will."

Dale, confused and not wanting to stand against Jim turned to Hinckley and said, "Tell him to write out that draft."

"No man," said Hinckley. "These boys have been wronged and deserve a settlement. But, I am not going to let you rob me."

"Then I'll just shoot you plain and simple," said Dale.

"You are not going to get any money by shooting me either," said Hinckley. "Just give it up and get on out of here while you are ahead, son."

Dale walked over to the couch where Cal and the woman sat. "Well," he said, " I'll tell you what. If Jim don't start writin' that draft right now al'm gonna ventilate this woman's head."

Dale thumbed the hammer back on his pistol and started to raised it, movement from Jim at the desk caught his attention. Jim had pulled a Colt from the desk drawer. Dale turned toward him. Jim fired, Dale fired at about the same instant. Smoke and the acrid smell of spent gunpowder filled the air from the two deafening explosions. Both men were hit. Jim went over backward in the chair, a wound to his shoulder. Dale stumbled backward a few steps and fell to the floor clutching his abdomen with one hand and hanging on to his pistol with the other. Blood gushed through Dale's fingers. Wild panic filled his eyes. He cocked the pistol and aimed at Hinckley.

"Yer gonna get yers now, you rich son..."

"NO," said Sam who had the Schofield drawn and aimed.

Dale brought his pistol around to fire on Sam. "I've had enough of you too" he said. The Schofield spoke loudly and Dale jerked from the impact of the slug. The pistol fell from his fingers and he melted into the floor motionless.

"Damn-it," Cal said.

"He gave me no choice," defended Sam.

"Yeah, I know it," said Cal. "I just hate that it had to happen this way."

Hinckley and Miss Priscilla rushed over to Jim who was bracing himself on the desk struggling to stand up. Priscilla examined his wound. "You will need to see a doctor to get that bullet out of there," she said. Then Hinckley and her sat Jim in the desk chair.

"Youngster," Hinckley said, "You had better help your brother and get out of here before Haze and that posse get down that hill."

"You mean yer still gonna let us go?" said Cal.

"Sure. Nothing has changed," said Hinckley as he picked up the draft made out to Sam and Cal and held it out to Sam. "Here take this and gather your brother and go. And, good luck to you boys, spend it wisely.

"By the way, I wouldn't be found around these parts for a mighty long time if I was you fellas."

"No problem Mr. Hinckley," Sam said as he took the draft from Hinckley's hand. "Me and Cal know of a ranch up in Colorado we can buy for a song. And that's where we'll be a headin'."

Sam went over and helped Cal hobble toward the door where they stopped. Cal hopped around to face Hinckley on his good leg. "I wanna thank you sir. You're a right fair man and I hope you do well from now on."

"Yes sir. I thank you too," Sam said. "So long."

"I'm glad I was able to compensate a little for your losses. Now get going before you lose your head start, youngster."

Sam tipped his hat to Miss Priscilla and helped Cal out to the waiting horses. They mounted and rode off through the mesquite bushes.

Sam and Cal became very successful ranchers in Colorado. Due to Carlton Haze's bad business practices the H&H Railroad went bankrupt not long after that. Over the loss of everything he owned, Haze ended up taking his own life with a .32 caliber pistol one night.

Hinckley, Priscilla and Jim had made some outside investments down in South America and after Bradley and Priscilla got married they all retired very wealthy people.

THE END

Made in the USA
San Bernardino, CA
10 September 2018